# COUNTDOWN

Ben Mikaelsen

**HYPERION PAPERBACKS FOR CHILDREN**

**New York**

By the same author

*Rescue Josh McGuire*
*Sparrow Hawk Red*
*Stranded*

First Hyperion Paperback edition 1997

Text © 1996 by Ben Mikaelsen.

A hardcover edition of *Countdown* is available from
Hyperion Books for Children.

24 23 22 21 20 19 18 17 16

The text for this book is set in 12-point New Baskerville.

Library of Congress Cataloging-in-Publication Data

Mikaelsen, Ben
Countdown/ by Ben Mikaelsen—1st ed.
p.    cm.
Summary: In two parallel stories, a fourteen-year-old boy who is NASA's first Junior
Astronaut and a fourteen-year-old Maasai herder in Kenya both edge into maturity
while questioning their family traditions.
ISBN 0-7868-0252-9 (trade)—ISBN 0-7868-2207-4 (lib. bdg.)
ISBN 0-7868-1208-7 (pbk.)
[1. Astronautics—Fiction.  2. Masai (African people)—Fiction.
3. Kenya—Fiction.] I. Title.
PZ7.M5926Co   1996
[Fic]—dc20
96-19998

V475-2873-0 13095

This book is dedicated to the
seven astronauts who lost their lives
aboard the Space Shuttle *Challenger*.

They died living a dream.

# ACKNOWLEDGMENTS

This book would not exist
without the help of a great many people.

*A special thanks to*

Loren Acton, Spacelab 2 Astronaut;
David Simonson, Operation Bootstrap Africa Director;
Barbara Yates, editor and friend;
James Mandras, U.S. Space and Rocket Center
Research Coordinator;
Patricia Moore, Payload/Crew Training Manager;
Jim and Cynthia Lefevre, editors and friends;
Nicholas Ole Matiko, Maasai guide and consultant;
the Marshall Space Flight Center, Huntsville, Alabama;
and the U.S. Space and Rocket Center, Huntsville, Alabama.

I found that the spelling of Maasai words varies greatly from source to source. I have tried to use the most commonly used spelling, however, the Maasai language of Maa is not easily adapted to English. For example, the plural of a Maa word can be a completely different word. To allow the reader to understand, I simply added the English *s* to a Maasai word to make it plural. Maasai people will recognize this as incorrect. These liberties were taken solely to facilitate communication. No slight was meant to the Maasai culture or language.

*"The first day or so we all pointed
to our countries. The third or fourth
day we were pointing to our
continents. By the fifth day
we were aware of only one Earth!"*

—*Sultan Bin Salman Al-Saud (Saudi Arabia), Astronaut*

# CHAPTER ONE

**B**itter wind from Crazy Peak tugged at the sagebrush as fourteen-year-old Elliot Schroeder coaxed his big buckskin horse back toward the ranch. He rode easily as if his short frame had grown from the saddle. Across his lap, he held a kicking newborn calf. The morning wind gusted. Elliot pulled an old gunnysack from his saddlebag and wrapped it around the bloody calf like a blanket. He clapped his frozen gloves against his pants to warm his hands and threaded his way down the rocky slope. The calf's mother followed, bawling her concern. The calf kept struggling.

"Knock it off!" Elliot scolded, squinting into the driving snow. "You'd be dead if I hadn't found you."

He was right, too. Early snows could freeze a calf to death before its mother licked it dry. Elliot knew he was lucky to find the calf. He had been daydreaming, watching the snowflakes swirl past him like stars past a spaceship blasting through space. Only the mother cow's bawling had caused Elliot to look down.

"Daydreamers wreck ranches," Dad often said. Elliot agreed, but imagination didn't switch off like a light switch. Even now, Elliot remembered every airplane and space poster taped up in his bedroom. He remembered each minute of every flight lesson he had taken during the past two years.

Each month he saved all of the money he earned so that he could ride his bicycle seven miles to the airport on the bluff above Big Timber for a flight lesson. He couldn't wait to solo an airplane. What would it be like being alone in the air the very first time? Elliot's thoughts never stopped there. He couldn't look up into a night sky without wondering what it would be like in space. Were there aliens out there somewhere? Thinking about space travel made Elliot giddy with excitement—especially since NASA had made their announcement!

One month ago, with his parents watching the evening news, Elliot had overheard the words that would change his life. With dozens of cameras whizzing and clicking at NASA Headquarters in Washington, D.C., a NASA spokesman had announced simply over the TV, "Ladies and gentlemen, tonight NASA is announcing the first Junior Astronaut program. Somewhere in this country, one youth will have the opportunity of space travel."

As reporters screamed questions, the man held up his hand and kept speaking. "Our grandparents dreamed of moving westward. We dreamed of landing on the moon. What do our children dream of?"

The man turned solemn. "Most children have no dreams at all. Drug addiction, alcoholism, teenage pregnancy, truancy, high suicide rates, juvenile delinquency, gangs—these are not dreams." The man paused. "Last year a special presidential commission convened to discuss the problem of rebuilding the dreams of the nation. Based on the panel's recommendation, NASA is today announcing the first Junior Astronaut program."

"You would risk a child's life?" asked a reporter.

The spokesman replied bluntly, "America did not become great by tiptoeing on dreams. Dreams don't come from a video arcade at some mall."

Even now, riding through the driving snow on his horse, Elliot remembered what was said next.

"Who will the child be?" shouted a reporter.

The NASA spokesman shuffled papers in his hands. "Selection will *not*, I repeat *not*, be based on exceptional aptitude or ability. *Every* youth in America *must* be able to share the same hope of becoming that first Junior Astronaut. For this reason, selection will be determined by a national lottery."

A stunned silence followed those words. The NASA spokesman continued quickly. "Application forms will be mailed to every school in the nation. Provided a student meets basic physical criteria, any child between the ages of ten and fifteen will have an equal opportunity to become the world's first Junior Astronaut. The goal is to rekindle a dream."

Elliot had turned his full attention to the TV and jumped to his feet. "Mom! Dad! Did you hear that? They're sending a kid into space."

Elliot's parents, Angie and Dalton, yawned. Dalton looked at his watch. "It's about time for bed, isn't it?"

"It could be me!" Elliot shouted. "It could be me!"

"They wouldn't send a fourteen-year-old who can't do homework," Angie kidded.

"Or chores," Dalton added.

"No, really!" Elliot said. "It could be me! I already take flying lessons." He pointed at the TV. "Listen!"

The NASA spokesman continued. "Some will say this plan is ludicrous—that taking a child into space will not revitalize a nation. We disagree. Tonight, after hearing this announcement, millions of children will go outside and look up. Tonight dreams *will* be planted."

Elliot knew one dream had been planted. That night after lights were out, he climbed out the window of his upstairs bedroom. Alone on the roof in the cold evening air, he stared at the sky until midnight. What would it be like to really blast off into space? The thought burned in his head like a hot ember. Two weeks later he was the first at school to turn in his completed six-page NASA application.

Some parents wouldn't sign the consent form. Most, however, were like Elliot's—they signed just to make their kids quit begging. "There's more chance of lightning hitting a mosquito," Elliot's dad joked, scribbling his signature.

Elliot pulled the calf against his Bulky Carhartt jacket as the barn came into sight. The mother cow still followed, bellowing her displeasure through the falling snow. Elliot was not thinking about the calf. He was thinking about tomorrow. Already NASA had held their lottery to choose the first Junior Astronaut and tomorrow they would announce the winner. Tomorrow lightning would strike somewhere. Why not here?

**AT THAT MOMENT,** fourteen-year-old Elliot Andrew Schroeder had no way of knowing how NASA's Junior Astronaut lottery would turn his life upside down. Nor did he have any way of knowing how the Junior Astronaut selection would change the life of one Maasai boy in Kenya, Africa.

As Elliot lifted the freezing newborn calf onto a warm bed of fresh straw, half a world away a young Maasai herder, Vincent Ole Tome, also lifted a newborn calf. He slumped it over his shoulders. The birth fluids darkened the red-striped toga sheet that covered Vincent's body.

Long shadows told the fourteen-year-old herder he must return to the *engang*, his family's cluster of dung huts. Vincent whistled to start the restless herd moving. He kicked a clod of dry dirt at the old cow that had given birth. Why did she wait until the moon was chasing the sun from the sky to have her young? Soon darkness would make the leopards, lions, cheetahs, and hyenas grow bold. Then nothing was safe.

Ahead, baboons chased across in front of the herd. Their sharp grunts broke the stillness. A mother baboon trailed behind the pack, her baby clinging tightly to her stomach. She angled toward the distant trees, avoiding a dead zebra carcass.

Life and death were brothers, Vincent thought. A lion had taken down the old zebra to give life to her newborn cubs. Life brought death, and death gave life. This is how it had always been—this is how it must always be. They should be equal.

But it seemed to Vincent that he had seen more death than life. Like an old man breathing less each day, the land also breathed less. Rains no longer came willingly. The tall honey-colored grasses Vincent remembered no longer grew. Carcasses of dead Cape buffalo dotted the horizon like termite mounds. Only the buzzards did not die. The fat birds hopped about, picking at the rotting meat.

Why was the land dying? This question made Vincent's forehead wrinkle in thought. Even the wildebeests were fewer. Once these shaggy beasts had come to Maasailand in such great numbers they had covered all the ground from sky to sky. All of the land seemed to move. Elders said the stars would fall to Earth before the wildebeests disappeared. And yet they were disappearing. They vanished from the land like water from a cracked drinking gourd.

Vincent had no answers as he drove the herd toward the small-huts of the engang that was his home. When finally he neared the engang, he stopped, the calf still across his shoulders. Vincent stared out across the valley from the engang to the shiny tin roof and the low grayed walls of the wood schoolhouse. He hoped nobody watched him. In Maasailand it was said that a wandering mind cannot protect a cow. The elders and warriors beat herders they caught dreaming or telling stories.

Still, Vincent stared. For two years his father, Tome, had allowed one of his sons to learn at the wood school. That son had been Vincent. It had cost three cows each year but the greatest cost to Tome had been losing the help of a son.

It was there at the wood school that Vincent's Maasai name, Ntoros, had been changed by the head-master to the white man's name, Vincent. Tome did not like the new name, but he allowed it. Then the rains had quit, and many cows had died.

Once again, Vincent was made to herd.

Staring at the wood school made Vincent's mind more hungry then ever. The land outside the school-house was cracked and dead. But inside, children from other engangs learned new ideas. Their minds thought new thoughts. And all Vincent could do was stand with a bloody calf across his shoulders and dream.

# CHAPTER TWO

**B**ack in the United States, Elliot Schroeder finished his chores, keeping an eye on the calf he'd brought in. The calf stood on wobbly legs and bunted at its mother for milk. The barn door swung open, and in walked Elliot's father, Dalton. Looking at the man, it was easy to see where Elliot got his blond hair. Dalton's weathered skin and lazy grin hid his age. His lips toyed with a stub of straw. "How's the calf doing?" he drawled.

"Great," Elliot said.

Dalton Schroeder grabbed a bridle for his bay gelding. "The wind's letting up. Let's head up to tree line and look for Old Crowleg. Fresh snow might be our ticket to finding that crafty old bugger."

Elliot nodded. For years he and Dad had been after this one old bull elk. It had seven points on each horn and was the biggest and smartest elk in three counties. They called the bull Old Crowleg because one front hoof angled in from an accident. Probably a hunter's bullet.

Dalton saddled his horse, and soon he and Elliot rode toward tree line, their rifles tucked in leather scabbards. "These snows might bring Old Crowleg down from the high country," Dalton commented, sitting tall in his saddle.

Elliot heard his dad speak, but he was busy thinking.

"You're sure quiet," Dalton said. "I swear, ever since you started flying lessons, your head has been somewhere else."

"I'm not thinking of flying lessons. I'm thinking of blasting off into space. Tomorrow NASA announces their first Junior Astronaut."

Dalton laughed, reining his horse up a draw. "There isn't a mosquito's chance in a tornado of your winning that lottery. Give it up and get your head back to ranching."

Elliot shook his head. "Even if I don't win, I still want to be a pilot someday and fly."

"You're better off here on the ranch."

"But, Dad, I don't want to ranch. I want to—"

"You think you're too good to ranch and get your hands dirty." Dalton spit the stub of straw from his lips and spurred his horse up beside Elliot. "Son, four generations of Schroeders made this place what it is. Where is your pride? You don't just walk away from this like a Sunday picnic that's over. How many kids ever get to ride in country like this, looking for an elk like Old Crowleg? He's special. You're special. This place is special."

Elliot said nothing. This argument always ended the

same way. But still, someday he wanted to do more than look at the sky and just dream of flying. He wanted to be a pilot.

At tree line, Dalton motioned. "You hike in here. I'll ride ahead and work back."

Elliot nodded and dismounted. He snubbed his horse to a tree, then walked into the woods with his rifle. Snow crunched under his steps. A squirrel raced along a deadfall, storing nuts for the winter. What Dad said about ranch life was true, Elliot thought. You would never find Old Crowleg in New York City. But you could never fly through the clouds sitting on a horse, either.

Among the trees, snow fell lightly. Elliot moved forward, angling up the slope. He picked each step. After a quarter mile, he leveled off and skirted the mountain, crossing each ravine cautiously.

Ahead, a porcupine waddled into the underbrush. Two whitetail deer flagged their tails and bounded upslope. Instinctively, Elliot froze. They had not run from him.

Long minutes passed. Finally Elliot started forward. At that same moment a branch cracked in the trees. Like a majestic ghost, a huge bull elk moved into the open at the bottom of the next draw. It was Old Crowleg. The elk hobbled slightly. His nose jutted forward, his huge horns tipped gracefully back.

Elliot stared at the proud and magnificent bull. Old Crowleg was probably moving away from Dad. As the bull approached, Elliot looked down at the rifle in his hands. Finally he raised the rifle and aimed. He did not slip off the safety.

Through the scope the elk appeared even bigger. Each breath pumped from the bull's nostrils like steam from a dragon. Elliot moved the crosshairs back and forth across the massive body. He hesitated, then clicked the rifle's safety off. He had seen Old Crowleg during the last five years, dozens of times—sometimes in the high meadows protecting his harem of cows, sometimes all alone in the thick deadfall. The bull always moved like a king.

As Elliot carefully shifted positions, his knee snapped a twig. Crowleg's head turned, muscles twitching. Still Elliot kept the rifle's crosshairs centered on the proud and powerful chest. He rubbed the trigger but did not pull. Finally he lowered the rifle. Crowleg grunted at the movement and crashed into the thick brush. As quickly as he had appeared, he was gone.

Elliot stared at the rifle in his hands. If Dad loved the ranch so much, and if Old Crowleg made this place so special, why shoot the big elk? It didn't make sense. Elliot shook his head. He didn't dare talk to Dad about things like this. Elliot trudged back toward the tree line to get his horse.

Dalton waited for him. "See anything?" he called as Elliot walked up.

Elliot shook his head. "Nothing worth shooting."

**VINCENT OLE TOME** arrived home at his family's engang before dark. In Maasailand, every family lived close together in small-huts made from cattle dung and built in a circle around the corrals. Maasai small-huts were so low one had to crouch to enter. Vincent's father, Tome, lived in the largest round hut. His three wives each had their own. Vincent and his younger brothers lived together in another small-hut. Nearby lived their grandparents. Across the engang lived Vincent's many sisters.

This night, the older sisters stacked more thorned tree branches around the corral—a lion had been prowling, stirring up the herds.

Vincent quickly placed the calf with its mother and herded the cattle into the corral. When he finished, he grabbed two chunks of goat meat and left the engang. Already the children filed into the small-hut of Grandma Natana to hear stories.

Spear and walking stick in hand, Vincent crossed the valley toward the far slope. All Maasai carried walking sticks—even the children. To not do so would let their arms swing like the white soldier. Vincent eyed the infirmary standing brightly on the far hillside. The infirmary held magic! Sick people were made well.

The Maasai doctor, Sambeke Ole Koyie, had been trained in Nairobi. He wore the clothes of the white man. He owned many things. One black object, called a microscope, allowed Vincent to see things that were invisible. Also, Sambeke had what he called a generator. When it roared loudly, a round glass glowed brightly. This magic, Sambeke called electricity.

Most magical to Vincent was the black box that

Sambeke spoke to. It was called a ham radio. Voices from all over the world spoke through the box to Sambeke. Vincent had learned English well at the wood school. Some English voices from the black box, however, sounded different and were hard to understand.

Vincent loved visiting the infirmary each evening. He helped sweep and mop the hard floor. Sometimes he helped pour medicine into thin glass containers. Everything brought new questions, new smells, new sights, new magic.

As Vincent approached the infirmary, he pulled his red-striped toga closer around his shoulders and idly pushed several fingers through the large hole in his lower ear. The holes had been cut when he was younger. With time he had stretched them large to make himself handsome. At the top of each ear, a short colored peg was pushed through a smaller hole. This also made Maasai people very beautiful.

Down the hill from the infirmary stood the wood school where Maasai children from many engangs learned new ways. They wore the white man's clothes, and many had no holes in their ears. The school filled Vincent with memories, with wanting, and with fear. They taught only in English, so when Vincent had gone, he struggled to learn the new language. The white headmaster frowned always, as if the look had dried on his face. He said the school was not there to teach the ways of the Maasai. Speaking the Maasai language, Maa, was not allowed in his school.

Once Vincent did something forbidden by the head-master—he tried to write in his own language, Maa, to see if ideas could be told this way also. For disobeying, Vincent was made to touch his forehead to the front desk while the headmaster caned him hard with a staff. Still Vincent's mind stayed hungry for new ideas. That is why he visited the doctor, Sambeke, this evening.

When Vincent arrived at the infirmary, Sambeke waved to him through the open door. "How is Dreamer Boy?" he called warmly. "You are late tonight."

Vincent smiled shyly. "A cow waited to give birth so that I could carry her calf all the way to the engang."

"See, cows are not so dumb."

"If they are not so dumb, why do they need the Maasai to keep them from becoming lion food?"

"A good riddle," Sambeke said, motioning Vincent inside. Sambeke's smooth black skin was not weathered and rough from being outside.

Vincent entered the infirmary, bowing in respect to his elder. Sambeke reached and touched Vincent's head gently as was the way of the Maasai. "Did you come to see more magic?" he asked.

Vincent nodded.

"Then tonight I will disappoint you."

"Why?"

"Because nothing here is magic."

Vincent frowned.

"Everything here has been made by people." Sambeke

pointed to his head. "People using their minds."

"But I do not understand these strange things."

Sambeke laughed. "Ah, so if Vincent Ole Tome does not understand, that makes it magic."

Vincent turned his head downward with embarrassment.

"Look, Dreamer Boy." Sambeke gestured about the small clinic. "What you see here was made by people like you."

"Not like me," Vincent said more boldly. "I have not gone to school long enough."

"You have gone to the wood school for only two years, but always you have learned the ways of the Maasai. Wood schools do not teach the ways of the heart." He motioned. "This generator cannot teach honor. My equipment does not teach pride." Sambeke lifted something from around his neck. "Can this stethoscope teach honesty?"

"What is that?" Vincent asked.

"Dreamer Boy, I think your stomach eats questions for food. Never have I found one with so many questions."

Vincent smiled. "You say that one cannot ask too many questions."

Sambeke returned the smile. "That is true, but sometimes you must find your own answers." He took the stethoscope and carefully placed it over Vincent's ears. The other end he placed against his own chest.

Wide-eyed, Vincent listened. Soon he heard a muffled beat like the galloping of a zebra.

"That is the sound of my heart," Sambeke said.

"How do you know?"

Sambeke shook his head in feigned frustration. "Magic," he said, laughing.

"There is no magic," Vincent said.

"Ah, the young pup learns to bark." Sambeke looked out the window at the darkening sky. "If you do not leave soon, you will share your walk home with the lions and hyenas."

"I wish I did not have to leave," Vincent said quietly.

Sambeke opened the warped door without answering.

Vincent nodded good-bye. "Thank you, Sambeke," he said. Reluctantly he headed back across the valley.

The day had left no light in the sky when Vincent reached the engang. Carefully, he pulled back branches placed at the gate to keep lions from entering. The restless sounds of hungry cattle drifted with the air. From Grandma Natana's small-hut came silence—already the young ones slept.

As Vincent placed the last branch back across the opening, his mother, Peninah, came to him. She was not his birth mother, but she was wise and often helped speak to Vincent's father when he grew angry. Speaking in their Maasai language of Maa, she said quietly, "Vincent, your father wishes to speak with you."

Vincent knew already why he was being called, and he thumbed the peg in his ear fearfully.

# CHAPTER THREE

In Montana, Elliot Schroeder awoke with a start. This morning NASA would announce the winner and the alternate selection for their Junior Astronaut program. "You dumb fool," Elliot thought to himself. "One chance in millions is the same as no chance at all." Still he found himself short of breath.

Haying the cattle took forever. So did breakfast and the six-mile bus ride to school in Big Timber. Elliot spotted a blue van parked near the front entrance in the No Parking zone. On the door were the words NATIONAL AERONAUTICS AND SPACE ADMINISTRATION. "NASA!" Elliot whispered.

Inside, the halls buzzed with excitement. Elliot ran to his locker. Could the winner be from Big Timber? He drew in a deep breath. Even if the winner was from here, that could still be any one of nearly a hundred students. Elliot dropped off his jacket and picked up his books. As the bell rang he slipped into his first-hour science class.

The teacher, Mr. Boyt, tapped on the desk for quiet. His voice sounded like someone had pinched his nose. "Okay, class," he began. "As you know, in less than one hour NASA announces the winning student of their Junior Astronaut program. I thought it appropriate to spend this class period discussing the implications of taking a child into space."

The teacher's words melted into a hum as Elliot stared out the window at the blue sky and what lay beyond. Were there other civilizations out there somewhere? Would they communicate with us?

"Elliot," Mr. Boyt said, "what do you think would be the result?"

Elliot jerked his head forward. "Uh, result? Result of what?" he asked, embarrassed.

As the class snickered, Mr. Boyt looked up at the clock. "Never mind, it's almost time for NASA's announcement." He snapped on a classroom TV. Elliot held his breath.

"NBC is going live to NASA Headquarters in Washington, D.C., at this time," announced a newsman.

The screen switched to a woman who was walking to a podium. "Good morning, ladies and gentlemen," she began. "Today it is my distinct pleasure to announce the winner and the alternate winner of the National Aeronautics and Space Administration's Junior Astronaut program." She opened an envelope in her hand.

"Should the winner become ill or fail physical flight exams, the alternate will be . . ." She unfolded a piece of paper and coughed. "The alternate will be Mandy Jane Harris of Allentown, Pennsylvania."

Elliot licked at his dry lips as the lady continued. "And the winner, ladies and gentlemen . . ." She took a breath and spoke louder. "The winner is . . . Elliot Andrew Schroeder of Big Timber, Montana!"

Elliot did not hear any more of the woman's words. A dull roar in his head scrambled his thoughts. As if in slow motion, everyone in the room turned to stare. Already Elliot felt weightless. He could not remember his name.

**YOUNG MAASAI HERDER** Vincent Ole Tome feared being called to his father's small-hut. "Papaa!" he called, nearing the opening.

"*Tijinga,*" came the command from inside, telling him to enter.

Vincent obeyed, crouching to enter the darkened hut. Smoke from the olive-wood fire hung as heavy as Vincent's thoughts. His father, Tome, sat gazing into the weak flames. Sweat glinted from his forehead, and he did not look well. For many days now, Tome had stayed inside his small-hut, eating little.

Vincent sat and waited without speaking.

Tome spoke in Maa with riddles and proverbs—this was his way. He said it helped Vincent learn the way of the Maasai. "Vincent," Tome began. "Are you clever?"

"Yes," Vincent said. This was how they always began.

"How clever?" Tome asked.

"As clever as a mongoose."

Tome nodded gravely. "We shall see. What crosses the wilderness without talking to you?"

"My shadow, Papaa."

"And how many kinds of trees are there?"

"Two, Papaa. The dry one and the green one."

"Which tree is cruel and hates all the others?"

Vincent thought. "I think it is the tree that is used for kindling."

Tome's face twitched from the thoughts that brought his riddles. "What moves across the world but leaves no trace?"

"The butterfly, Papaa."

"Vincent, you have learned well, but the ways of the Maasai are so many they can never all be learned."

"I know this, Papaa."

Tome worked his mouth as if chewing on his tongue. "The zebra does not shed its stripes. The elephant does not grow tired of its tusks. So why do you grow tired of being Maasai?"

"I am not tired of being Maasai, Papaa."

"You speak always of the wood school. Are not the ways of the Maasai your school? I see you look at the sky as if to keep blood in your nose. And every night you visit Sambeke."

"Papaa, Sambeke is Maasai. Visiting him is not wrong."

Tome shook his head. "A lion goes most often to the place it finds food. Is the food of the Maasai not enough for this young lion? Sambeke does not teach the ways of the Maasai."

"Papaa, all that is around me I wish to learn."

"So, you learn the ways of the rat," Tome snorted. "Someday you will come back. When a rat grows hungry, it returns home."

"I do not leave home."

"You do not hunt lions and elephants and buffalo with the boys who wish to be warriors."

"Papaa, Sambeke says the laws of Kenya say it is wrong to kill the lion and the elephant."

Tome spit into the fire. "Maasai know only the laws of the Maasai!"

"Much is changing. Sambeke says that all people, even the Maasai, must change or they will be destroyed."

"To change *is* to be destroyed. My son, a log on the hearth laughs at the one in the fire, and the coals laugh at the ashes. Is the Maasai ash? Is this why you speak of going to the wood school? You think the Maasai is ash?"

Vincent shook his head. "No, Papaa. The wood school teaches things the Maasai do not know."

"And the Maasai teach things the white man does not know. How can you hold a spear in one hand, a herding stick in another, and also books? Do you have three hands? My son, I do not teach you so that you may hate me."

"I do not hate you, Papaa. I will always love you."

"To stay together is to love each other. That is the wish of our god, Engai."

"Papaa, nobody should disobey Engai, but I think—"

"Engai made the Maasai," Tome interrupted. "It is her wish that we be Maasai. She did not make us jackals. Engai should not be tested." Tome coughed again and again as he poked more olive wood into the coals.

The small fire grew, making the air more hot. Vincent stared at the curling yellow flame, fearing the next words from his father.

Tome stopped coughing and said, "Soon there will be the ceremonies of *Embolata Olkiteng* and of *Alamal Lengipaata.* These will help you to become a warrior."

"Papaa," Vincent pleaded. "My heart wants to—"

"The thread should follow the path of the needle," Tome said forcefully.

Vincent bit hard at his lip. "Papaa, please let me learn at the wood school. I will still be Maasai. I do not need to kill a lion or an elephant to be Maasai."

Tome kicked at the coals, sending sparks dancing up into the low dung ceiling. "The donkey stands beside the cattle," he spit. "When they are watered, the donkey also gets drink. When they are grazed, he, too, gets grass. But he is still a donkey. My son will become a warrior and not a donkey.

"You cannot protect Maasailand if you do not have courage. Tomorrow when the other boys from this valley hunt to prove their courage, you will go with them." Tome looked up at Vincent, his eyes glinting with sickness and anger. "I have not raised a donkey or a coward!"

Vincent stood and left quietly. He did not allow the tears in his heart to come to his eyes.

O n the TV, the words were repeated. "The winner of NASA's Junior Astronaut lottery is Elliot Andrew Schroeder."

Elliot's mind struggled with the name. It must be someone else. It must be. Some other Elliot Andrew Schroeder had won the Junior Astronaut lottery.

The classroom door opened, and in walked the principal, followed by a man and a woman in blue suit coats with NASA lapel patches. By now all the students were standing and cheering. Elliot couldn't speak. His face felt hot. He had trouble swallowing.

"Are you Elliot Schroeder?" asked the NASA man, pushing past the frenzied students.

"I guess," stammered Elliot.

The man shook Elliot's hand vigorously. "Congratulations, son. I'm Frank Boslow." He gestured. "This is Ms. Jackie Lopez."

Elliot felt like a fish gulping on air. "Uh, I can't believe it."

"Believe it, son," said Mr. Boslow. "Your parents are on their way here right now."

"This is crazy," Elliot said, dumbfounded.

"Sit down, everybody!" shouted Mr. Boyt as students pummeled Elliot. Others jumped up and down, whistling, clapping, and hooting. Elliot's mind clogged with questions.

"Come!" shouted the principal, guiding Elliot past the clustered students and down the hallway. Cheering erupted from other classrooms as they passed. When the door closed behind them in the principal's office the noise finally grew muffled. For the first time, Elliot took a better look at the two NASA people.

Ms. Lopez had dark hair and looked trim in her NASA jacket. Elliot liked her warm smile and big dark eyes. Mr. Boslow was older and more rumpled. His jacket looked too small for him. He had bushy eyebrows that looked like worn-out toothbrushes, and he talked loudly. "What does it feel like to be selected as NASA's first Junior Astronaut?" he said.

"Dad told me there was more chance of a mosquito getting hit by lightning," Elliot said.

Ms. Lopez laughed and held up a thick folder. "When your parents arrive we'll go over these forms. You must have a million questions."

Elliot nodded. "How soon will I go into space?"

"In nine months. NASA wants you on the STS-97

mission aboard the Space Shuttle *Endeavour*. Training will be based at the Johnson Space Center in Houston, Texas."

"I still can't believe it," Elliot stammered, shaking his head to wake himself from the crazy dream.

"One million dollars will be spent on your training," Ms. Lopez explained.

Mr. Boslow clapped Elliot on the back. "The million-dollar man."

"The same will be spent on your alternate, Mandy Harris," Ms. Lopez added.

"A girl?" Elliot said, remembering the alternate announcement.

Ms. Lopez nodded. "Yes, a girl!"

Elliot scratched at his leg. "Do I get to skip school?"

The principal leaned back in his chair. "Your training will be the greatest school on earth. Or in space. Imagine all you'll learn."

A knock on the door made Elliot turn. In walked his parents. Dalton and Angie still wore their work jeans and flannel shirts. Uncertainty clouded their faces. "Is it really true our son has been picked to go into space?" Dalton asked.

"Sure is, Mr. Schroeder," answered the NASA man, Frank Boslow, introducing himself and Ms. Lopez.

Angie hugged Elliot, worry creasing her forehead. "We'll have to talk about this. I don't know if you should go into space."

"Mom!" Elliot exclaimed, "I've already been picked."

"Elliot's right," said Dalton. "This was all settled back when we agreed to let him enter the lottery."

"But it could be dangerous," said Angie.

"I'm not afraid," Elliot said, squaring his shoulders.

Ms. Lopez tapped a pencil deliberately on the table and studied Elliot. "You should be," she said.

Elliot coughed nervously. "How soon do I start training?"

"In three days we'll fly you to Houston," Ms. Lopez said. "You'll have a week of briefings and orientation. Then it's down to business!"

"He can't go to Houston alone," Angie said.

Ms. Lopez seemed surprised. "Of course not. We encourage you to move to Houston during Elliot's training."

Dalton looked directly at Elliot. Frustration edged his voice. "Tending a ranch doesn't allow us to run off to Texas for nine months. We'd have no ranch left when we came home."

"Elliot will be well cared for and supervised," said Mr. Boslow. "Once he starts training, he will be busier than a pigeon in a hurricane. Time will be extremely limited. NASA is risking a lot with this program."

"We're risking our son," said Angie.

Ms. Lopez smiled understandingly. "I know it won't be easy for you two."

"Mom and Dad, I'll be all right," Elliot said.

"Are you sure of that?" Angie asked, hugging Elliot.

Dalton grumped, "He'll be fine. It's us that will be

train wrecks." He turned to Elliot. "Just make sure you come back from space so I have someone to take over the ranch."

Elliot avoided his dad's eyes.

For two hours Elliot and his parents sat in the principal's office asking questions. Finally Mr. Boslow looked at his watch. "We've arranged a news conference in the gym at eleven-thirty. It's almost time."

As they walked toward the gym, Elliot looked out and saw the parking lot jammed with cars. In the gym, students and townspeople filled the bleachers—half of Big Timber was there. Elliot's mom and dad were given front-row seats among the press. Ms. Lopez and Mr. Boslow joined Elliot at a table set up in the middle of the gym floor.

For an hour, reporters questioned Elliot. At first they asked things like, "How does it feel?" and "Are you excited?" But then one lady with lots of makeup stood and asked, "Why should money be wasted sending you into space when people are starving in the ghettos?"

Elliot shrugged. "Maybe the information we get will help people," he said. "Besides, with me in space, you'll have one less down here." He didn't mean to be funny, but everybody laughed. The lady sat down in a huff.

A big man with puffy red cheeks stood and said, "By sending you into space, isn't NASA really trying to get funding from Congress for other projects like the Space Station or a Mars mission?"

Elliot shrugged. "I don't know what NASA thinks," he said. "I haven't talked to them, but I do know this." Elliot pointed to all the students. "If your Congress won't approve the money for a Mars mission, someday ours will."

The students in the auditorium clapped and whistled.

Mr. Boslow stood, ending the news conference. He turned and shook Elliot's hand. "You'll do just fine as NASA's first Junior Astronaut."

Ms. Lopez nodded her quiet agreement.

Elliot wasn't so sure.

**MAASAI HERDER** Vincent Ole Tome walked slowly from his father's small-hut and around the cattle corral to the hut he shared with his younger brothers. Carefully he rested his spear outside. Inside, everybody slept. Vincent kicked the cow-skin sandals from his feet and lowered himself onto the stiff cowhide to sleep. The cold night air carried the restless sounds of the cattle.

Vincent listened. When the stomping and hungry bawls did not stop, he rose and crept out into the open air. Maybe it was only the cattle's hunger, but maybe they smelled a lion. He picked up his spear.

Moving as silently as a cheetah, he walked to the edge of the corral and crouched in the dark. Listening and waiting, he gazed up. Why did the rains not come to the great Maasailand? Had something chased them from the sky? Each day the angry clouds gathered and churned but then left again without letting the forgiving rains fall from their great white bellies.

The elders prayed to Engai, the one and only god. But this did not stop Engai's anger. Yesterday the elders had picked a sheep of only one color and killed it. They burned the body in the shadow of Mount Lengai, a holy place. The smoke from the fire had risen, proof that Engai received the offering. But still the rains did not come. Why was Engai mad?

Vincent stared at the black sky filled with stars. He knew the sky well because he looked up often. But one does not understand all that one sees. For Vincent, the more he looked up, the more it brought questions to his head.

Some elders believed that stars were the eyes of the God, Engai. Vincent searched for the three stars that stood in a row. These were the three elders. The stars about them were the widows wanting to marry the elders. Farther down in the sky waited Vincent's favorite star, *Leken*, the bright star of the evening.

The elders searched the sky each night for Leken as a sign of rain. Also they searched for *Inkokua,* the group of stars that always brought the heavy rains. This year the Inkokua had forgotten to bring rain. Now the elders searched for any good sign, even shadowed rings around the moon.

A cow bawled, and Vincent searched the dark corral. Something bothered the cattle. If a lion attacked the cattle at this moment, he would take his spear and kill the lion. One life would end to save another. Vincent understood this balance. But tomorrow Papaa had demanded that he hunt lion or elephant with the boys from the other engangs, killing only to prove courage. Vincent did not wish to kill in this way.

But he could not stop tomorrow's sun from rising.

Later, when the cattle had quieted and the stars were tired of being watched, Vincent rose and returned to the small-hut. His head hurt from not finding answers. Still, the night would not let him sleep. His thoughts moved among the stars, among the eyes of Engai.

Early, with the sun still hiding, five boys came from other engangs. Obediently, Vincent left with them. He carried his spear, his walking stick, and his *knobkerrie*, a short branch with a polished knot on one end. This worked well for prodding cattle if held by the knob, or for fighting if held by the shaft.

"How many lions have you killed, Vincent?" asked Leboo, the tallest and loudest of the boys.

"None," Vincent admitted quietly.

Leboo poked Vincent with his knobkerrie. "Ah, then the lions know you are a coward."

The other boys laughed.

Vincent remained silent.

"Going to the wood school has made you a coward," Leboo taunted. "What kind of name is Vincent?"

When Vincent still did not answer, Leboo spit at the ground. "A jackal does not become a warrior. Why do we take a coward to help kill the lion Olarani?"

Olarani was the name given to one old male lion who had grown very large and escaped many hunts. His name meant "killer."

Leboo pointed at Vincent. "If you make more noise than my shadow, I will throw my spear at *you*." He turned to the rest. "I have seen Olarani by the river where the valley narrows. He grows old and sleeps much. I think today he will die."

In a single line the boys walked. They would not reach Olarani until the sun rose high. Vincent pulled his red-striped toga tightly around his shoulders. The red sheet could be seen from very far in Maasailand. This was how it should be. All living things should fear the Maasai.

As the boys neared where Leboo had last seen the great lion, Olarani, they spoke more and more boldly. "Today we will make a kill," said the boy Mosipa.

"I will throw the first spear," bragged Leboo.

Vincent remained quiet. He feared Olarani. All boys feared the great lion. But Vincent's fear did not make him hate the big cat. If it attacked his herd, then, yes, he would try to kill it. But why kill Olarani for no reason?

As they neared the river, all talking stopped. Only the trees and the wind made sounds. If Olarani was here, each boy would try to be the first to spear him. This brought great danger because lions remembered well. Though attacked by many spears, lions tried always to kill whoever brought the first pain.

After throwing spears, the next honor came to the one who first grabbed and held to the great Olarani's tail.

"There," whispered Korio, a short boy with big muscles and a slanted smile. He pointed to a pride of lions resting in the shade of an umbrella tree.

"Where is Olarani?" hissed Leboo. "He must be near. I think these are his lions."

The boy Siparo pointed. "There . . . by the water. He hides near the black tree far from the others."

Siparo was right. It was the great Olarani.

Staying far from the main pride, Vincent joined the boys as they surrounded the big lion. The great Olarani lay in the shaded grass and raised his shaggy yellow head to watch them. As they closed in, he rose stiffly to his feet and gazed about with his head held low. His whiskers twitched.

One step at a time the circle tightened, each boy with his spear held over his shoulder. Olarani's great chest filled with air and he bared his teeth, sounding a deep and chilling growl of death.

# CHAPTER FIVE

**I**n Montana, Elliot Schroeder's life shifted suddenly into high gear. At the ranch, the phone rang nonstop, even after midnight. Finally, Elliot's dad jerked the cord from the wall. "This is a ranch, not a zoo," Dalton grumped.

At breakfast, Elliot's mom, Angie, commented, "This is the first time I've ever fed an astronaut."

"No it isn't, Mom." Elliot grinned. "Before, you just didn't know I'd be going into space."

During the next three days, NASA arranged television interviews and a big parade in Big Timber. The last day before leaving, Elliot saddled his horse, Cooper, and rode one last time up into the foothills. When he neared tree line, he stared up into the snowy canopy of trees. His breath showed in the crisp fall air. "Good luck, Old Crowleg," he whispered; then, reluctantly, he returned home.

Back at the ranch, Elliot pulled off the saddle and

rubbed down his horse. He patted Cooper. "Good-bye, old boy. I won't be seeing you for a bit."

Cooper nuzzled Elliot's cheek.

After final packing and lunch, it was time to leave. Elliot's parents rode with him in the pickup. His father whistled low as they pulled into the airport. "Look at that!" He pointed at a private jet parked on the ramp, not far from the Cessna 150 Elliot used for lessons. Across the jet's shiny white tail were the letters N-A-S-A.

"This is awesome," Elliot said breathlessly. "That thing is huge compared to the Cessna 150. Can you believe it? I'm riding in a private jet!"

Dalton poked Elliot. "Get used to it, hot dog."

Under a deep blue Montana sky, with hundreds of townspeople gathered, Elliot said good-byes. The high school band was there, playing "America the Beautiful." Elliot hugged his parents hard. Finally, Angie and Dalton let him go. Concern showed strongly in their eyes. "Remember where home is," Dalton said.

Elliot nodded and headed for the plane. The chief pilot welcomed him with a handshake. "I understand you're headed for space, young man."

Elliot squared his shoulders. "I hope so, sir."

"We'll be flying you to Houston. If you need anything, let us know. Feel free to visit the cockpit."

"You don't mind?"

"We'd be honored," said the pilot, showing Elliot to his seat behind Ms. Lopez and Mr. Boslow.

"This is unreal," Elliot whispered aloud, as he

settled into the large cushioned seat. He pushed his face against the round window and waved at the cheering crowd.

After takeoff, Elliot slumped back. Until now, adrenaline had kept him pumped and awake, floating emotionally outside himself. But now climbing up through the clouds, he had time to really think. Fear settled in and gnawed at his gut like a ranch rat chewing on a sack of grain. He was actually doing it. He was on his way to the Johnson Space Center to be an astronaut!

The jet's flight path shadowed the east side of the Rockies south toward Texas. Over southern Colorado, Elliot stood and worked his way forward to the cockpit. The pilots greeted him. "This is the business end of a Gulfstream jet," the copilot said.

Elliot stared at all the instruments, radios, switches, and lights. This sure wasn't a Cessna 150.

"Want to fly her?" asked the copilot.

Elliot grinned. "I couldn't fly this thing. All I've ever flown is a Cessna 150."

The copilot slid from his right seat. "This crate really isn't much different."

Cautiously, Elliot sat and gripped the yoke. With coaxing, he pulled back and pushed forward. Then he steered left and right. The big jet climbed, dived, and banked.

"Hey!" yelled Mr. Boslow from the back. "You guys want my lunch on the floor?"

Elliot grinned and steered more gently. "What is this

instrument?" he asked, seeing one he didn't recognize.

For an hour the pilots explained the cockpit. Elliot kept a close eye on the rate-of-climb indicator, the airspeed indicator, the altimeter, the turn-and-bank indicator, and the compass. He even helped change radio frequencies.

"We'll soon be starting our descent into Ellington Field," said the standing pilot. "Unless you plan on landing this bucket of bolts, you better let us take over."

Elliot slid from the seat. "Thanks," he said. "Thanks a million."

"You'll make a fine astronaut," said the head pilot.

Elliot nodded and returned to his seat. He hoped the pilots were right. He still couldn't picture himself as an astronaut. His insides felt like a balloon getting ready to burst. What would it feel like to be weightless?

**RELUCTANTLY** Vincent Ole Tome helped circle the great lion, Olarani. As the boys moved slowly closer, the boy Leboo began a low mesmerizing chant. The others joined in until it sounded like a swarm of bees.

The great Olarani spun, raking the ground with his claws and exploding forward with short vicious charges. His powerful muscles bulged and rippled under his shiny yellow coat. The chant droned louder. Olarani's eyes glinted. His rumbling growls sounded like thunder from the earth.

Without warning, Leboo raced in from behind and flung his spear. The thin shaft pierced Olarani's side. The lion's thundering roar stopped the circle of boys.

Olarani spun, biting at the spear and breaking the wood shaft. Half the spear still stuck into his body. The boys closed again as Leboo ran quickly outside the circle to hide. Olarani would charge Leboo now if he saw him.

The boy Tinga ran in next and speared the great Olarani's neck. Again Olarani roared, biting at the spear. Then he chased Tinga. Immediately Mosipa and Korio closed from the side and threw their spears hard. Olarani stumbled and pawed at the ground. Life from his body left long red smears on the dried and cracked ground. The boys' chants rose like the howling of the wind. The chilling sound mixed with the lion's hollow growls.

Olarani collapsed. Mosipa bent low and crept in, grabbing the big lion's tail to show his courage—he would get to keep the tail. Olarani grunted and swatted weakly. Siparo ran forward and buried his spear deep in the cat's heaving chest. This brought a last gurgling roar, and then Olarani lay still except for the twitching of his paws.

The boys cheered wildly, all except Vincent. Leboo saw Vincent still holding his spear and ran up to him. "You are more than a coward," he screamed. "You are goat dung. You are an earless dog." Leboo spit in Vincent's face and grabbed his spear. He ran over and threw the spear into the lifeless Olarani. "Vincent is a coward." Leboo shouted again. "But his spear is not."

Vincent wiped his face and watched quietly as the

boys worked cutting off claws, ears, and tail to prove their bravery. Overhead, the vultures circled. When the boys started back, Vincent walked over and pulled his spear slowly from the butchered body. The blade glowed red with blood. There were no grasses to wipe it clean. The ground was too hard.

At that moment, Vincent understood one reason why the great Maasailand was breathing each day one less breath. This death came not from the anger of Engai. This death came not from their enemies, the Kikuyu and the Kissii. Nor had it been brought by the white man. This death had been brought only by the Maasai, and this death would bring life only to the vultures and the hyenas.

# CHAPTER SIX

**W**hen Elliot's jet stopped on the tarmac in Houston, a white van pulled alongside. The whine of the jet's engines slowed as the door was opened. Elliot coughed on the hot humid air that rushed in.

Mr. Boslow pointed. "The van will take us to the Johnson Space Center. Let's get you settled into crew quarters and introduce you to Vaughn Kelso, our director."

"You'll meet alternate Mandy Harris, too," Ms. Lopez added.

Elliot nodded as they loaded into the van. He didn't say anything, but already he'd made up his mind—nobody was taking his place in space, especially not a girl.

Elliot's home at crew quarters was a small apartment with a kitchen, a living room with a TV, and a bedroom. After unpacking, Ms. Lopez handed Elliot a green security badge. "Put this on," she said. "It allows you access to most buildings here."

"Your training will be as a payload specialist—an astronaut who is trained for one specific mission only," Mr. Boslow kept explaining as they drove to the administration building. "Besides standard Orbiter training, you'll be trained to run the SAREX radio. SAREX stands for the Shuttle Amateur Radio Experiment."

"Great," said Elliot. "I've used my dad's CB radio in the truck."

"You'll also assist with life-science experiments."

"What's that?"

"How space affects the physiology of a growing adolescent," Ms. Lopez explained. "They'll test your muscle and bone loss, blood volume and pressure, heart size, spinal changes, space sickness. Those kinds of things."

Mr. Boslow laughed. "You'll be a human guinea pig."

"Will I get shots?"

Mr. Boslow nodded. "And blood tests."

Elliot smiled weakly.

"This is the administration building," said Ms. Lopez, stopping beside a large concrete building with flags out front. As they walked in, she said, "Elliot, you live in such a wonderful place. The space center's high-tech world will be so different."

"I can't wait," Elliot said.

Ms. Lopez smiled. "Get ready to have your life scrambled."

Inside, a guard checked their identification and badges. Uneasy, Elliot twisted at his sleeve as they rode the elevator.

"Vaughn Kelso is director here at the Space Center." Mr. Boslow winked at Elliot. "So mind your manners."

"Just be yourself," Ms. Lopez advised.

Elliot was ushered into a big waiting room where a secretary greeted them. Near her desk, on a leather couch, sat a girl with straight brown hair. She was short and sturdy, with knee-length shorts and thick white ankle socks. Her freckles and dancing eyes made her look mischievous.

Elliot couldn't stop the feelings that welled up inside. This was his once-in-a-lifetime chance. He had always dreamed of space. This was his chance to be the very first Junior Astronaut in history. No freckle-faced girl in dumb-looking white socks was going to take that from him.

Spotting Elliot, the girl stood. She smiled and extended her hand. "Hi, I'm Mandy Harris."

Elliot shook her hand. With a guarded voice he said, "I'm Elliot Schroeder."

"I'm so excited and happy for you!" Mandy said.

Elliot didn't believe her for a second. How could she be happy someone *else* was going up instead of her?

"Mr. Kelso is free now," announced the secretary. "Please follow me."

Everyone filed into a huge office with windows on two sides overlooking the Johnson Space Center. At a desk sat an old man with a thin face, wire-rimmed glasses, and a baggy suit. He looked like someone's grandfather. He gazed at Mandy, then at Elliot. "So, you're Mandy and Elliot, the spacekids," he said, adjusting his glasses.

Elliot nodded nervously. He didn't like Mandy's name being mentioned first—*she* was the alternate.

"You can relax," said the man. "I'm Vaughn Kelso, just one of the workers here at NASA."

"They said you were the director," Elliot ventured.

Vaughn Kelso pulled a small gold chain from his desk drawer. He handed it to Elliot. "Do me a favor, son," he said. "Show me the most important link in that chain."

Elliot puzzled. "Uh, sir, they're all important,"

"Right." A slight smile parted Mr. Kelso's lips. "History remembers Neil Armstrong for walking on the Moon. But he wouldn't have stepped off a curb without help from thousands of others equally as committed. We're all links in a chain. We're a team. If you fail a task or assignment, you fail the whole team. Do you understand?"

Elliot nodded.

Vaughn turned to Mandy. "As mission alternate, don't think you are less important than Elliot. Our intent is to place one of you two into space nine months from now aboard the STS-97 mission. It's not important which one of you goes up. What's important is the mission." Mr. Kelso drummed a pen against his desk. "Do you *both* understand this?"

Mandy nodded eagerly.

Elliot nodded, but he knew he could never let Mandy or anybody else take his place as the first Junior Astronaut. This was his one chance in life to be somebody.

By the end of the first day, Elliot swore he had met every human being at the Johnson Space Center. At times he was too overwhelmed to think. Mandy Harris laughed, smiled, and acted sweet to everyone, as if it were a big party.

Later, when they went to a fancy restaurant in downtown Houston, Elliot watched Mandy spread her napkin neatly on her lap and eat small bites with her fork upside down. Elliot left his elbows on the table and chewed hard. "I'd starve eating like that on the ranch," he said.

"It's a good thing we're not at the ranch," Mandy said plainly. Later, leaving the restaurant, she looked up at the sky and said, "Elliot, can you believe it? We're really going to be astronauts!"

"Yeah," Elliot said. He didn't say what he really thought.

Back at crew quarters, Elliot called his mom and dad. The sound of their voices made him homesick.

"The coyotes killed a calf yesterday," Dalton said.

Elliot felt guilty for not being there. He told his parents how big and frightening everything was at the Johnson Space Center. He didn't say anything about

Mandy. All too soon the phone call ended, and Elliot crawled into bed.

When the alarm rang at six o'clock the next morning, Elliot felt like a sack of lead. He stumbled around getting ready, shaking sleep from his head. Today they started physical examinations and what was called pre-orientation.

After a quick breakfast, Elliot and Mandy were measured for jumpsuits and pressure suits. Again, Mandy wore her thick white socks. She raised her arms expertly and helped position the tape as her measurements were taken. Elliot couldn't wait to see how she did once training started. Becoming an astronaut wasn't the same as eating politely or getting measured for clothes.

"Now the real fun starts," Mr. Boslow said. "You begin physical exams."

The exams began with eye tests. Because special eyedrops made their pupils big, Elliot and Mandy left the exam wearing cheap plastic sunglasses to guard against the sun. Next they filled out about a zillion forms and answered two zillion questions. Then a lab woman drew blood using needles big enough for knitting. Wide-eyed, Elliot watched as six tubes of blood were taken from his arm. "Are you feeding a vampire?" he pleaded.

Nobody laughed. Mandy closed her eyes and turned her head away from her own ordeal.

Elliot didn't feel well anymore.

A thin man with a white coat led Elliot into a small office. For two hours he took notes and asked weird questions like, "Do you like yourself lots, some, or little?" Or, "If a close friend fell through thin ice, what would you do?"

That question was easy. "I'd throw out the lariat I always carry on my horse, Cooper," Elliot said.

"And if you didn't have a lariat?" the examiner asked.

Elliot chuckled. "Then I'd probably jump through the ice, too. It's better than the whupping I'd get from Dad for not carrying a rope out calving."

The thin man thought before making notes on that one.

When the questions ended, the man stood abruptly and said, "That will be all."

To finish the day, Elliot and Mandy were strapped into spinning chairs. Both ended up getting sick. As they left, Elliot told the doctor, "I'm glad this is over."

The doctor glanced up from his notepad. "Oh, this is just the beginning. Wait until the life-science people from Ames Research Center get a hold of you."

Elliot looked to see if the doctor was kidding. He wasn't. A big lump wedged in Elliot's throat. Suddenly, going into space didn't seem like such a hot idea.

**VINCENT OLE TOME** returned slowly to the engang. The other boys walked far ahead. They laughed and sang, holding up the lion's claws and ears, and bragging loudly of their kill. Mosipa swung Olarani's tail in circles over his head.

For Vincent, the journey to the engang ended too soon. Already word of the hunt had spread, bringing quiet and accusing stares. Only Vincent's favorite mother, Peninah, spoke to him. "How was my son's day?" she asked quietly.

"Mamaa, the boys killed a lion, but I did not help."

"Why did you not help?"

"The lion was the great Olarani. Today he did not attack the cows—he slept beside a tree."

"Has not Olarani attacked cows before?"

"That is when he should have been killed." Vincent gestured. "Today, Leboo, Korio, Tinga, Mosipa, and Siparo, have killed Olarani without thinking of the cows."

"But did they not prove their courage?"

Vincent shook his head. "There were many of them and only one Olarani. That does not show courage."

"So, how do *you* show courage?"

Vincent stabbed the ground with his spear. "If Leboo had thrown down his spear and grabbed Olarani's tail while he slept, that would have shown courage."

"I think that would have shown he was foolish."

"He has already shown that many times."

Peninah smiled gently. "Today your father is angry at even the air he breathes. Maybe some old-man's meat will make him happy. Go kill a goat."

Vincent rested his spear against the engang and entered the small pen of goats beside the corral. This chore he did not like. With a quick movement he grabbed a thin black goat and held its nose tightly.

The goat struggled for air. Vincent looked away toward the disappearing sun until he felt the last jerks of the small body. Maasai killed goats this way so that no blood would be wasted. Vincent pinched the soft nose a while longer, then carried the limp goat to Peninah's small-hut.

Peninah drained the blood into a hollow gourd. This calabash of blood she mixed with milk for drinking. The hide she saved for drying. Bones would make jewelry and knife handles. Meat and fat she would cook later.

Vincent squeezed dung from the long intestines and from the lower stomach. He smeared the sweet-smelling brown paste on Peninah's small-hut to fill cracks. The intestines he boiled in a pot for soup. Peninah pulled out the tender liver and cut off pieces for herself and for Vincent. Hungrily they ate. She handed the rest to Vincent. "Here, give this to your father."

Vincent obeyed. The raw liver was called old-man's meat because it could be eaten by the elders with no teeth. Near Tome's small-hut, two of Vincent's youngest brothers chased each other, laughing and throwing dried cow dung at each other.

"Papaa!" Vincent called, approaching Tome's small-hut.

"Tijinga," answered Tome from inside, his voice cracking.

Vincent crouched and entered. He searched the

darkness and bowed. Tome reached weakly and touched his head. "Peninah sent this for you, Papaa," Vincent said.

Without speaking, Tome took the old-man's meat. His hands shook. His skin looked stretched over his bones. As Vincent turned to leave, Tome said, "Sit by the fire."

Obediently Vincent sat.

"Are you clever?" Tome mumbled.

"Yes," said Vincent, fearing the words not yet spoken.

"How clever?"

"As clever as a four-legged chair that does not walk."

"What is it that smokes but cannot be lit?"

"Fresh cow dung," Vincent said.

"Who has the smallest nose?"

"The safari ant, Papaa."

Tome stared into the fire. His body swayed as if blown by a wind. "What object can never be overtaken?"

"My shadow, Papaa,"

Tome sucked in a long shallow breath. "Your shadow is like the will of Engai. She brings the rain and the sun and the darkness. Engai has made you Maasai. Like your shadow, this you cannot change."

"I do not wish to change the will of Engai, Papaa."

"You visit Sambeke, but you do not honor your spear and hunt for lion?"

"Papaa, Sambeke shows me things the Maasai do not know. Someday all Maasai will know what Sambeke knows."

"Bark from one tree does not stick to another." Tome struggled with his words. "You know well the words of the Maasai, but words are not dust that blows with the wind. Words should catch in your mind like the ox hair catches on the thorn."

"Papaa, Sambeke says the Maasai will not last if they do not change."

Tome spit into the smoldering olive-wood fire. "The ways of the ancients are the ways of the Maasai. They teach us good and bad. The white man is the one who will not last because he forgets the ways of the ancients." Tome spit again at the fire and scoffed, "Sambeke is not Maasai. He is a jackal who laughs at the moon."

Silence hung like a heavy cloud. Tome's voice had grown weak. He motioned for Vincent to leave. "Words do not touch your mind. They only bounce from your ears like chunks of goat dung."

Vincent stood silently and left.

After his father's angry words, Vincent Ole Tome slept with troubled thoughts. He rose early. Already his mothers Nasha and Noonkishu worked in the morning's still gray air. They stood inside the corral holding up a bony young cow that swayed about on wobbly legs. The heifer's head hung low. Her eyes were dull with weakness.

Vincent ran and leaned against the living skeleton, poking the heifer with his elbow. If the animal fell down, it would die.

"She cannot be helped," Noonkishu said finally. "Bring the arrow and bleed her."

Vincent returned with his bow, a blunted arrow, and two calabashes to hold blood. The animal would be bled so that she died more quickly and so that more of her blood could be saved and mixed with milk for drinking later.

While Nasha held the heifer's head, Noonkishu held on to the tail. Vincent drew back the dulled arrow with his bow and pierced the heifer's neck. Slowly the calabash filled with squirting blood. The heifer dropped to her knees, then collapsed onto her side. Vincent slashed her neck with a knife and filled another gourd. The last blood would pool in the chest to be dipped out later.

"Go now and herd the cattle," Noonkishu said to Vincent. "We will cut up this cow."

Vincent looked at the herd. They were wild-eyed with hunger, bawling, milling about, crowding each other, and pushing their heads over each other's backs.

Peninah came to the corral holding a small calabash filled with soured milk and fresh blood. She handed the gourd to Vincent.

"Thanks, Mamaa," Vincent said.

Peninah nodded and walked silently to the opening of the corral. She pulled aside the thistle branches that kept out wild animals. Overhead, wind and dark clouds troubled the air.

With his herding staff and spear in hand, Vincent

prodded the cows forward. They were angry and clumsy with weakness. The wind swirled dust into small funnels that danced out ahead of the herd. There were fifty-five cattle, but Vincent did not need to count them—Maasai herders knew their herds so well that missing cows were like missing friends.

Today would be hard. Until the cattle found grazing, there would be no rest. Vincent knew that short grasses lined the dried streambeds a morning's walk away. He drove the herd forward. Whistling, yelling, and swinging his staff, he moved side to side to keep the herd bunched. Whenever a cow lunged from the herd, Vincent ran fast, striking the cow to drive it back. Cows obeyed only if the pain from his stick was greater than the pain already chewing at their empty bellies.

When not crazy with hunger, a herd moved slowly like water flowing in a stream. This herd churned like a flood, twisting and fighting. Vincent worked to keep the restless herd clear of any death smell. Dead buffalo covered with vultures only made the herd more crazy. Today, even the smell of ostrich droppings brought fear.

Baboons crossed in front of the herd, babies clinging tightly to their mothers' stomachs. Vincent listened for the loud barks that sounded whenever baboons grew scared. Often, baboons warned of leopards.

Two elephants passed nearby. Zebras and Thomson's gazelles dotted the bare hills. Even without rains, the land held life. Death of buffalo brought life for lions and vultures. Death of gazelles meant life for the cheetah.

That was what made man different, Vincent thought. Man brought death but gave little life in return.

When small patches of grass appeared, Vincent allowed the cattle to chew the dry blades. He sipped from his calabash and thought of Leboo's angry teasing. Was it wrong to not help kill the great Olarani?

The troubled day passed slowly, bringing thunder but no rain. The thunder made the cattle drunk with fear. Finally Vincent's long shadow warned him it was time to return to the engang. As he turned to whistle at the cattle, a deep growl chilled the air. A twig cracked.

There was no other warning.

A streak of yellow flashed from nearby shrubs and leaped onto a cow. The cow bawled as a lion bit into her neck. The herd churned in confusion.

Vincent ran directly at the lion. He flung his spear hard, piercing the lion's hip. The lion screamed and let go of the cow. She bit at the spear, pulling it loose. Again she attacked the cow.

Vincent picked up his spear and swung it hard across the lion's nose. The lion snarled and pawed at her bloody face. Spinning, she charged at Vincent.

Vincent stood ready. When the lion leaped, he flung his spear into the lion's shoulder. He closed his eyes and ducked sideways. Her chilling growl filled the air as a big paw struck Vincent and tore skin from his back.

The lion ripped the spear from her shoulder with her mouth, breaking the wooden handle like a twig. Long smears of blood streaked her body. She snarled one last time, then turned and ran. Her long yellow tail flicked a shrub like a whip, then she disappeared.

Heart pounding, Vincent stood. His back burned with pain but he did not think of himself. The attacked cow lay dying. Something else was wrong. Without counting, Vincent knew two more cows were missing. He looked. In every direction stood bushes that could hide the missing cattle.

Vincent chanted softly to the herd as he searched. It was no use. Already his shadow had grown too long. Sadly, he walked up to the injured cow and ended her suffering with his broken spear. Overhead, vultures circled. Vincent knew that by tomorrow only the cow's scattered bones would remain. He shouted loudly—he would have to drive the cows hard to reach the engang by dark. Holding his broken spear in one hand, he swung his staff and whistled.

Vincent's worst fear had come true, and he shivered at the thought. Already Papaa was angry. Now his son returned home to tell him that three cows had been lost. Three cows. They would have paid for one year of learning at the wood school.

# CHAPTER SEVEN

**D**uring orientation, Elliot and Mandy flew from coast to coast, touring NASA's facilities. They wore blue jumpsuits everywhere. Mandy always wore bright white socks.

"Don't you have any other color socks?" Elliot asked, as they were shaking hands at NASA's headquarters in Washington, D.C.

"I wear white for good luck," she said.

"That's silly," Elliot said.

At that moment, a guide met them. She stared at Elliot and Mandy very seriously as she began her talk. "Let me put things in perspective. Energy churned out by the Sun has always been the main cause of change on Earth." She raised her hand as if preparing to cast a spell. "But no more!" She pointed around. "Man is breeding and multiplying like pack rats. Feeding, clothing, and housing these billions of new people is changing our planet more than any sun."

She paused awkwardly, her eyes intense. "Earth is a spaceship hurtling through space. We cannot leave Earth when it fills up or becomes a garbage heap." Her voice sounded sad. "People take better care of their cars than they do their planet. Your mission will help us learn how to care for this spaceship we call home. Do you understand?"

Both Elliot and Mandy nodded hesitantly.

After a tour of NASA's headquarters, they flew to the Goddard Space Flight Center in Maryland. From Maryland, they flew to the Langley Research Center in Virginia. The man leading that tour was a real brain. "This is NASA's oldest center," he announced. After that, he might as well have spoken a different language. Without taking breaths, he droned on and on with information like, "Major technical areas here at Langley are theoretical and experimental dynamics, materials and structures, space mechanics, and advanced hypersonic engine research."

"This guy's a robot," Elliot whispered to Mandy. "Who programmed him?"

She covered a giggle with her hand.

After a night at Langley, they flew to Wallops Flight Facility in Virginia. They watched a small test rocket fired into the upper atmosphere. "If you'd been here last week," said the guide, "you could have watched a four-stage Scout."

"That's one of their rockets that goes into orbit," Mandy whispered.

"I know that, Einstein," Elliot answered.

After a night in Virginia, they flew to the Stennis Space Center in Mississippi. Under blustery skies, they watched the test firing of a Space Shuttle main engine on a gigantic concrete test pad. Elliot grinned as he watched the blinding flames and steam. The roar echoed louder than any thunder. As the firing ended, a drizzling rain fell.

The guide held his hands up to the rain. "This is because of the test firing."

"I don't understand," Elliot said.

"Hydrogen and oxygen cause water vapor," Mandy whispered.

"I was talking to the guide," Elliot snapped. He was getting tired of this know-it-all girl with thick white socks.

"I was just trying to help," Mandy blurted.

The guide looked at them. "Is there a problem?"

"Not with me," said Elliot.

Mandy turned away.

After stopping at the Lewis Research Center in Ohio, they flew on to the Marshall Space Flight Center in Huntsville, Alabama, where they saw a mock-up of the Spacelab that fit in the Orbiter's cargo bay. They also watched scuba divers help astronauts simulate zero gravity in a huge water tank.

The last stop on the East Coast was at the nation's first spaceport, the Kennedy Space Center in Florida. Elliot had never seen anything in his life like the Vehicle

Assembly Building. It was a massive five-hundred-foot tall box, so high that sometimes clouds formed inside and caused rain. It covered as many acres as a small hayfield. The guide said the VAB could hold three Empire State Buildings.

On the launchpad, the Space Shuttle *Atlantis* stood poised for blastoff. Mosquitoes from the marshes nearby swarmed as thick as dust. The guide pointed at the towering white bullet-shaped rockets on each side of the Orbiter. "Those are the Solid Rocket Boosters, or SRBs—the world's largest bottle rockets," she said. "They're as tall as the Statue of Liberty and weigh three times as much. They cause the blinding flame and thick white smoke during takeoff." She handed them bricks of rubbery material. "This propellant is mixed in huge six-hundred-gallon bowls and poured directly into the SRBs' big metal casings to cure."

"Like baking a huge cake," Mandy said.

Ignoring her comment, Elliot swatted at mosquitoes.

The guide pointed up. "When those SRBs ignite, you feel like you've been rear-ended at a stop sign by a dump truck." The guide smiled at Elliot. "Still want to go?"

Cautiously, Elliot nodded.

The guide continued. "The Orbiter has its own engines that also help boost it into orbit. During climbout, they generate more power than twenty-three Hoover Dams." She pointed to the large rusty-looking tank attached to the SRB. "That's the Orbiter's external tank. Fuel flow from that tank to the Orbiter during climb-out would empty a swimming pool in twenty-five seconds."

"Does the Shuttle use regular gas?" Elliot asked.

The guide shook her head. "It needs something with a bit more kick."

Mandy glanced at Elliot and said, "That's why it rained during the test firing. The tank is filled with hydrogen and oxygen."

"That's right," said the guide. "The fuel would freeze your hand if you touched it."

Elliot glared at Mandy. Back at the ranch, he could show this know-it-all brain a hundred things she didn't know. She didn't know how to help pull a calf at birth or call in a bugling elk in the rut. How many bum lambs had she saved? How many sick critters had she sat with all night in the barn? And yet, here in Florida, she made him feel like a dunce.

The guide pointed. "That Orbiter is big enough to carry a school bus into space. It operates as a booster at launch, as a spacecraft in orbit, and finally as an airplane on landing. It's a hundred times more complex than any airliner."

Elliot had always imagined the shuttle as just a big plane of sorts. Standing here, he realized he'd be riding a small skyscraper into space. And this skyscraper could easily blow up, just like the Shuttle *Challenger*. An invisible hand squeezed at Elliot's chest.

To finish the tour, they flew to California and visited the Dryden Flight Research Center at Edwards Air Force Base, the Jet Propulsion Laboratory in Pasadena, and the Ames Research Center at Moffett Field. At Ames, Elliot met the team that would run medical tests on him.

The weeklong whirlwind tour ended near dusk back at Ellington Field near the Johnson Space Center in Texas. Elliot yawned hard. He hadn't been this tired since staying up all night with sick calves.

Leaving the jet, Mr. Boslow turned to them. "Well, kids, now the work begins."

**VINCENT OLE TOME** ignored the biting pain in his back from the lion's attack. Shifting winds and hunger had made the herd even more wild as Vincent struggled to drive the cattle toward the engang. He knew of herders who had lost all of their herd. For this, forgiveness came hard. Even the loss of three would bring punishment. This was the way of the Maasai.

Dust from the herd rose like a cloud as they neared the engang. The bloodred sun already touched the ground. Vincent wrapped his red toga tightly around his injured back. Children near the engang played hand games with chunks of charcoal. They looked up and waved.

Vincent's mothers Peninah and Nasha came and prodded the troubled cattle into the corral. They knew without being told that three cows were missing.

Vincent explained what had happened. Peninah nodded. Nasha frowned with doubt. Vincent did not tell of his injury. Truth held no honor if it needed proof.

"Tell your father what has happened," Nasha ordered.

Vincent nodded—this he did not need to be told.

Vincent found his father, Tome, sitting outside the small-hut, a wildebeest fly whisk in his hand. So sick was Papaa that sweat beaded his forehead even in the evening's cool air. He swatted at flies Vincent could not see. Vincent bowed in respect until Tome reached and weakly touched his head.

Vincent swallowed hard. "Papaa, a lion has attacked the herd. It killed one cow. Two more have run away. I cannot find them."

Tome studied Vincent through reddened eyes. "This lion, did you kill it?"

"Two times I threw my spear, but the lion did not die. She ran away."

"*Where* did you lose the cows?"

As Vincent explained the place, he saw Peninah working beside her small-hut. She glanced up, but Vincent knew she could not help him.

Tome stood. Fighting pain, he entered his small-hut and returned with a thin stick. He stared at the bloodied and broken spear still in Vincent's hand. He did not see the torn skin under Vincent's toga. "How do I know the blood on your spear is not from a rabbit?" he asked.

Vincent blinked. "Because I have told you it was from a lion, and I do not lie."

"You know the ways of the Maasai," Tome said.

Vincent nodded. Without being told, he bent forward at the waist and waited. Sickness had not made Tome's arm weak. He raised the stick. Ten times he struck Vincent's back. Each blow drove the pain of the lion injury like a spear into Vincent's body.

Vincent bit his lip to hold back his screams. He stared at the ground. Each blow brought new thoughts to his head. He thought of Sambeke and of the wood school. He remembered taking honey from the bees' nests without being stung. He remembered a time when questions did not fill his head. He remembered a time years ago when he still wished to be a warrior. These and many more things he remembered.

When the caning stopped, Tome slapped Vincent's head with his hand. "I strike your head because your mind does not think." Next he swatted Vincent's ear. "I strike your ear because it will not listen."

Vincent spoke strongly. "Papaa, I have done no wrong!"

Tome glared at Vincent. "My words do not find your ears. You think only of Sambeke and of the wood school. You do not think of the cattle. A dog cannot guard two homes. Go! Leave the engang! Go! Find another place to guard."

Tome sat heavily on his stool. The heads of peeking children ducked behind the small-huts. Vincent knew not to speak again. He turned and walked away. This caning had not been as hard as many given in

Maasailand. The greatest pain came to Vincent's heart because Papaa had not believed him. Now Vincent knew he must leave the engang. Only when a respected elder asked Tome for forgiveness, only then could Vincent return. This was the way of the Maasai.

Peninah came to Vincent's small-hut as he made ready to leave. She brought a calabash of milk and blood to drink. "There is nothing so bad that it cannot be forgiven," she said softly.

"I have done no wrong," Vincent said.

Peninah put a finger to her lips. "Shhhhh. In three days' time, come to me. I will find an elder to speak to your father."

Vincent moved stiffly from the pain.

Peninah touched Vincent's shoulder. "Are you hurt?"

Vincent clutched his toga tightly. "My hurt is inside." Without speaking, he left the engang and walked across the countryside toward Sambeke's. In his hands he carried all that was his; a knobkerrie, a walking stick, and his broken spear.

The night had chased away all of the day when Vincent reached the infirmary. The generator machine growled, making the lights glow brightly inside. Vincent knocked.

"Tijinga," Sambeke called.

Vincent entered.

Sambeke sat at the table with the black box. He turned. "Dreamer Boy, it is late. Do you like tempting the lions?"

Without speaking, Vincent approached to have his head touched, then he turned his back and let the red toga fall away to show his injuries.

Sambeke stared at the claw marks and the deep welts from the caning. "Vincent!" he exclaimed, standing. "What has happened?"

Quietly Vincent explained. "Now Papaa has sent me away from the engang," he said. "I have no place to go."

"You have this place," Sambeke said. "Sit. I will treat your back."

Vincent sat quietly until Sambeke returned carrying two bottles, some white cloth, and a tube with a needle.

Vincent had seen Sambeke use big needles to put medicine into people's arms. Now Sambeke used such a needle to fill a tube with medicine that looked like water.

"I do not need that!" Vincent insisted. His stomach wanted to give back his last meal.

Sambeke smiled and wiped a strong-smelling cloth over Vincent's arm. "This shot will keep you from feeling worse."

"Killing a mongoose does not make it feel better," Vincent pleaded.

"This will not kill you. Look toward the door."

Vincent turned his head away and closed his eyes tightly. He felt Sambeke pinch the skin on his arm, and then it seemed that a bee had stung him. Vincent turned to peek. Sambeke was pulling the needle from his skin. The air felt hot. The chair seemed to tip.

Sambeke squeezed Vincent's neck gently. "You are

not afraid to fight a lion, but you fear a small needle."

"The needle did not attack the herd," Vincent mumbled, squirming. "The Maasai do not use needles."

"If you do not like the white man's ways, then why did you come here?" asked Sambeke, as he cleaned the wounds.

Biting his teeth against the pain, Vincent did not answer. He thought about the white man's ways. They were so different. At the engang, the *oloiboni* and the *paangishu* used herbs and chants to heal. But the healers' medicine did not always help. Vincent let a thought come from his mouth. "Sambeke, Papaa says the white man will not last."

"Why does he say that?"

"He says the white man has forgotten the ways of the ancients."

Sambeke nodded. "What he says is true."

"Will the Maasai last?"

Sambeke shrugged. "The Maasai are like bull elephants. Many arrows do not bring them down, yet they trip over a creeping plant. Change is the creeping plant that makes the Maasai fall. The wisdom of the ancients is still in our heads, but there is much we refuse to see."

Vincent puzzled. "So change is not good?"

"Change comes like the morning sun—no one can stop it. But one can guide it. Because many white people have forgotten the ways of the ancients, change has become a mad elephant they no longer control." Sambeke paused, placing a bandage over Vincent's deepest gash. "Tell me, what does your father say about me?"

Vincent looked down. "He says you are not Maasai."

Sambeke spoke firmly. "In my heart, I will always be Maasai. A zebra does not lose its stripes because it walks a different path." Finishing, Sambeke motioned toward the black box on the table. "Before we sleep, does Dreamer Boy want to talk to someone far away?"

"Someone like me?"

Sambeke shook his head. "Change is a wind that blows differently on everyone. You will speak to someone touched by very different winds."

"Who, Sambeke? Who?" Vincent asked excitedly.

"Dreamer Boy, how do you fit so many questions into your mouth? Sit, we shall see who."

# CHAPTER EIGHT

In Houston, each minute was scheduled—not for one day but for the whole nine months until launch. Already Elliot hated all the rules and having to do everything with Mandy. She was nice enough—that was part of the problem. She seemed to get most of the attention, as if *she* were the first Junior Astronaut.

She was a brain, too. The second night back at the Johnson Space Center, Ms. Lopez asked at supper how much someone weighed in orbit.

"That's easy," said Elliot. "Zero. If you weighed anything you wouldn't float around."

Mandy thought, then shook her head. "You weigh almost as much as on Earth."

"Then why do you float?" Elliot challenged.

"You don't float—you fall like a sky diver," Mandy said. "In orbit you're always falling toward the Earth, but because you're going so fast, you go around it. You feel like you're floating because the Shuttle is falling, too."

"You're crazy!" Elliot said.

"She's right," Ms. Lopez said, smiling. "If you weren't orbiting at over seventeen thousand miles per hour, you would fall to Earth. You have to go far beyond the Moon to be truly weightless."

It made sense after being explained, but Elliot kicked himself for not figuring it out. That night he dreamed he was back in the mountains of Montana. He dreamed that Mandy was there and that he had saved her from a grizzly bear. She wouldn't be such a hotshot out in the woods.

After two weeks of training in Houston, Elliot had his chance to be in the woods. He and Mandy flew to Washington State. For three days, instructors taught them wilderness survival. Together they learned to follow compass courses, start fires, make shelters, purify water, find food, and use first aid. Mandy still wore her silly white socks.

On the fourth day, a helicopter dropped them off with one of the instructors deep in the backcountry. As the helicopter flew away, the tanned instructor, Mr. Gallagher, turned and spoke. "Okay, listen up. This is all I'm going to say. Pretend I'm not here. I will not help in any way unless your life is being threatened. I have supplies for my own use. You must find your own food and shelter. Your mission is to make it back to training headquarters." He pointed. "That peak is

Summit Peak. You each have a knife, a map, a compass, water tablets, and matches. Don't look to me for help. Beginning now, I do not exist!"

Those were the last words the rugged-looking man uttered. Elliot smiled to himself. Mandy might be a brain at everything else, but out here she was just a scared city girl. He pulled out his compass and map, found Summit Peak, and oriented himself to north. Mandy watched.

When Elliot had his bearings, he pointed south. "Training headquarters is that way seven miles.

Hesitantly, Mandy said, "I don't know much about this stuff, but look." She pointed to closely drawn lines on the map. "We have to cross these if we go straight. The instructor said the topographical lines show how steep the land is. These lines are so close it looks like a cliff."

"Topographical lines!" Elliot muttered. "Now you're talking like an expert at this, too. It's not a cliff. Probably just a steep hill." He pointed at the map. "I'm not hiking extra because you're afraid of a measly hill."

"We'll have to go twice that far if it is a cliff."

"Do what you want," Elliot said. "I'm going straight."

The instructor watched quietly.

"We need to stay together," Mandy said. "I'll follow you if you really think you're right."

Elliot folded the map and started walking. "I know I'm right."

They hiked for hours, stopping to drink from streams. The secret to survival was avoiding dehydration. Whenever they stopped to eat wild berries, the instructor ate sandwiches and granola bars from his pack. Late that afternoon they broke out of the trees into a saddle of land between two peaks. Beyond the saddle, stretching as far as each peak, a sheer cliff dropped nearly a thousand feet.

Elliot stared in numbed disbelief. How could there be a cliff? All day they had hiked over rolling hills.

Mandy said nothing, she just stared at the ground and scuffed her hiking boot against a rock.

"Go ahead," Elliot said. "Say I told you so!"

"We better head back," Mandy said quietly.

The instructor sat on a rock looking around as if nothing were wrong.

Angrily, Elliot turned and trudged toward the tree line. Now they would have to hike back two miles, then go around the cliff. Mandy followed, watching. The instructor trailed along behind.

After hiking a mile in silence, Mandy caught up to Elliot. "I'm not mad at you," she said. "You didn't know it was a cliff. We still have to make it to training camp as a team. We can do it."

Elliot didn't want to be a team with this know-it-all girl. He ignored her and kept walking.

By sundown they reached a ravine skirting west around the cliff. They made camp beside a stream. A school of trout scattered from the shallows as they approached.

"I'll start building a shelter," Mandy said.

"You probably don't trust me now," Elliot said, "but the sky is clear to the northwest. I don't think we'll get rain. We could sleep on pine boughs near the fire. I've done that lots of times up hunting."

Mandy nodded. "I agree. Besides, in a real emergency, we should keep a fire going for searchers to find us."

"It's not *we* going up in the Shuttle," Elliot muttered as he headed out to gather firewood.

"Quit pouting," Mandy said loudly. When Elliot didn't answer, she called, "I'll collect berries for supper."

Still Elliot did not answer—he had his own plans. After collecting wood, he whittled a spear from a pine branch and hiked upstream. He found a spot where the water rippled over rocks. Telltale shadows glided under the surface. Crouching, Elliot flung the spear hard. It stuck firmly into the sandy bottom. Fish splashed and raced for deeper water.

Elliot pulled his spear from the bottom and moved farther upstream. Again he found flat ripples and threw his spear at the fish. Again they splashed away. Elliot wished they were spawning—he'd be able to get much closer. He laughed. Mandy was probably thinking he was lost. Silly girl!

After resharpening the tip of the spear, Elliot found a new stretch of ripples. This time when he threw, the water boiled, and the spear flopped sideways, quivering. Elliot ran splashing into the water and shoved the spear against the bottom to keep the fish from wiggling off. He ran his hand down the shaft and gripped the fish's gills. Holding his catch up, Elliot chuckled. Mandy could have her berries.

Elliot pulled out his knife and waded to shore to clean the fish on a rock. It would be better to leave the head and guts away from camp in case a bear came sniffing around.

Mandy stood waiting beside a large fire when Elliot arrived back. The instructor crouched near his tent, a rain tarp extended out as a windbreak. He glanced over as Elliot entered camp. Elliot held up the fish. A glimmer of surprise showed in the instructor's eyes.

"You got a fish!" Mandy exclaimed, her shirt stained from collecting berries.

"Now we can *really* eat," Elliot said. Poking the fish with the spear, he held it over the flames. Patiently he turned his catch until the skin turned crispy brown.

"I'm starved!" Mandy said.

"Then let's dig in." Elliot cut the fish in half. Using flat river rocks for plates, they stuffed themselves on fish and berries.

The instructor finished his own supper and crawled into his tent. With nightfall, Elliot and Mandy stretched out beside the fire on beds of soft, sweet-smelling pine boughs. They had only light jackets for cover, but the crackling fire kept them toasty.

"We did ourselves proud tonight," Elliot said.

"I agree," said Mandy. "Good night, Elliot."

Elliot grunted good night.

During the night each of them got up and stoked the fire. Only when the wind tugged at the flames did Elliot notice the heavy clouds blotting out the stars. He pulled his jacket tighter around his shoulders and went back to sleep. The wind picked up more. Then big drops of rain started plunking down. Elliot and Mandy sat up.

"Hurry, let's stoke the fire," Elliot said.

That instant, the sky opened up with sheets of icy rain. Elliot and Mandy scrambled to stack wood on the fire. Finishing, Elliot put his finger to his lips and motioned for Mandy to follow. Drenching wet, he tip-toed through the downpour over to the nylon wind-break stretched forward from the instructor's tent. Mandy followed hesitantly. Barely had Elliot crawled under, when the zipper on the tent opened. Without a word, the instructor reached out and yanked down the windbreak, pulling the nylon sheet inside. Again the zipper closed.

Elliot sat on the ground, scowling up through the driving rain at Mandy. Flashes of lightning brought deep rumbles of thunder. The wind blew harder. "He's a jerk!" Elliot whispered.

"Let's find a tree," Mandy said.

Together they stumbled into the black night searching.

"There's a big one," Mandy said, pointing.

They ducked under the long branches and sat with

their backs against the trunk. Huddled shoulder to shoulder, they shivered in the dark.

Mandy poked Elliot. "So, are we having fun yet?"

**VINCENT OLE TOME** sat eagerly in front of the black box at the infirmary. "How can a voice travel far without being loud?"

Patiently, Sambeke explained how radio waves worked.

"So, these radio waves, why can I not see them?" Vincent asked.

"They are invisible. But to a ham radio, they are not." Sambeke spoke into the handset. "Calling CQ for any calls. This is 5Z4XZ, does anyone read me?"

A crackle of static was followed by a faint but distinct, "Go ahead, 5Z4XZ. This is VK2LDQ."

For a long while Sambeke spoke to a man who lived in a place called Australia. The Australian man spoke English very differently than anyone Vincent had ever heard before. After saying good-bye and turning off the radio, Sambeke explained how it could be day in a far-away country and still night in Africa.

Vincent did not understand how this could be.

Sambeke yawned. "I work tomorrow. Come, let's make a place for you to sleep." Sambeke shut off the loud generator and locked the infirmary door. A short walk into the dark night brought them to a small-hut with tall flat walls like the infirmary.

Never before had Vincent entered Sambeke's small-hut. It was very large. Vincent did not have to bend over to go inside. Sambeke lit a lamp and pointed to a thick sleeping mat that was held above the floor by squared chunks of wood. "That is your bed. Sleep on your stomach so that your back can heal."

Vincent nodded, carefully sitting on the bed. He peered at the strange things around him. "Sambeke," he asked. "Why do you do everything above the ground? You sit, sleep, eat, and work away from the ground. What is wrong with the ground?"

"Dreamer Boy, you would ask questions until the sun returned if I let you. Sleep. This day has brought plenty for your dreams. Tomorrow I will open my ears to your questions again." Sambeke shut off the lamp and entered another chamber of his big small-hut.

Vincent lay on his stomach. He closed his eyes, but his mind was kept open by thoughts and questions. Outside, the screaming bawl of the monkeylike bush baby split the still night. The sound did not help Vincent sleep as it did at the engang. Here there was not the sweet smell of cow dung and the thick smell of the olive-wood fire.

When finally the night grew old and tired like an aging elder, sleep captured Vincent and brought more thoughts to his head. He dreamed first he was a Maasai warrior, walking tall and proud across Maasailand. Smiling girls watched him and whispered to each other. Then suddenly he became a sneaking jackal with no tail. Vultures pecked skin from his back. Vincent awoke to find himself lying on his back in Sambeke's small-hut. Stiffly he rolled again to his stomach.

Vincent slept until the sun made the air warm. He awoke, feeling guilty for having slept so long. Already Sambeke had left. Vincent's back burned like fire as he pulled his red sheet stiffly around his shoulders and walked to the infirmary.

Low benches filled with people circled the mud-and-rock building. These were some of the Maasai whose sickness the oloiboni's herbs could not heal. Many more Maasai could be helped but they were too stubborn, Vincent thought. Stubborn like his father.

There was much to be learned from the ways of the white man. This Vincent believed. But also there was much the white man could learn from the ways of the Maasai. Many of the oloiboni's herbs *did* heal. Why did the white man not come to learn and be helped?

Sambeke greeted Vincent when he entered. "Has Dreamer Boy finished dreaming?"

Vincent hid an embarrassed smile. "Sambeke," he said. "Why does the white man not come to the Maasai to learn the ways of the ancients? They could learn many things that machines cannot teach."

Sambeke examined Vincent's back. "The Maasai say that a house cannot be fixed while the owner is still destroying it," he said, pulling Vincent's toga back around his shoulders. "The white man is still destroying his house. Now, let me ask you a question. Have you come to help?"

"Yes. What can I do?"

Sambeke showed Vincent how to wash and steam the shiny instruments used on patients. Later, Vincent cleaned the windows and swept the infirmary. He even swept leaves and stones from the red dirt outside.

When the sun climbed higher, Sambeke took Vincent back to his square small-hut to eat. Instead of meat, milk, and blood, Sambeke ate something made from grain. He called it bread. Also he boiled a seed-like food called rice. Vincent had never eaten this kind of food. He said nothing, but eating food that grew from the land was not the way of the Maasai. That is why the god, Engai, had made the goat and the cow. Those who ate food from the earth were laughed at and called Potato Maasai. Today Vincent felt like a Potato Maasai.

After eating, Vincent returned to the infirmary with Sambeke. He helped Sambeke until the last person had left. That night, Sambeke let Vincent talk on the ham radio. Vincent still could not believe the voice from the black box came from very far away. He looked out the window, but nobody was there.

That night Vincent slept better. He enjoyed being with Sambeke, but he missed his brothers and sisters, his mothers and his father. He would be happy when three days had passed so that he could return home. Three days was a long time to be without forgiveness.

# CHAPTER NINE

Drenching rain fell. Elliot sulked as he shivered next to Mandy under the large pine tree. This was his fault. He'd insisted they hike toward the cliff. Then he suggested not building a shelter. "Your white socks didn't bring us much luck this trip," he said.

"You didn't give them much of a chance," Mandy said.

When finally the rain let up, Elliot and Mandy crawled out from under the tree and returned to the fire. In the darkness, only smoking coals remained. Elliot stirred the coals and blew on them. Finally a small flame licked up. They broke up wet branches and laid them gently on the flames. After much effort, a smoky fire sputtered alive.

"This was all my fault," Elliot muttered, holding his wet hands close to the small fire.

"No, it wasn't," Mandy said. "I agreed not to build a

shelter. Once I agreed, then it was *our* decision."

"I don't want to talk about it," Elliot said, adding more wood to the struggling flame. He missed the ranch and his parents and his horse, Cooper. He missed everything he loved.

Elliot and Mandy hung their shoes and socks up to dry, then tried to sleep again. They squirmed to get comfortable on the wet pine boughs. "Half of me is warm, and half is cold," Elliot complained.

"Then on the average you should feel pretty good," Mandy said.

"Real funny!"

"Elliot, why are you so mad?"

Elliot didn't answer. With every word to Mandy, he felt he was hurting his chances of becoming the first Junior Astronaut. He wasn't being a team player, but what else could he do?

After tossing and turning for hours, they sat up and crowded near the smoldering fire. The night ticked by slowly, one second at a time. When the sky finally lightened, Mandy yawned and stretched. "Let's get going," she said. "If we don't, we'll be out here another night."

"Brilliant deduction," Elliot mumbled. He stood and dipped water from the stream onto the hot coals with his baseball cap. Nearby, the instructor rose and broke his camp.

As they started walking, Elliot turned to Mr. Gallagher. "I hope you slept *real* good," he said.

The instructor kept his stony silence, chewing on a granola bar as if no one had spoken.

"I'm starved," Mandy said.

"*He* sure won't give us anything," Elliot said loudly.

"We'll find more berries."

"I'd eat a dead rat right now."

Mandy wrinkled her nose. "Oh, gross!"

They shivered as they hiked. Finally the morning sun climbed, warming the air. By noon it had grown hot. They trudged along silently, stopping often to drink from streams. No matter how many berries they ate, it didn't help. Elliot couldn't remember ever being so hungry.

Mandy stopped and pointed at a small flat-leafed plant. "They said we could eat those roots."

"Go ahead," Elliot said. "I'm not a lizard."

They kept walking and walking without finding food. Late that evening, sunburned, blisters on their feet, and totally worn out, the two Junior Astronauts stumbled into training camp and collapsed on the ground. Their instructor approached, as fresh as when he started. "Okay, let's discuss what happened," he said, looking at Elliot. "First there was *no* teamwork."

Elliot sat sullenly.

"Second, what would have happened if you had needed to hike a hundred miles?"

"We'd have made it," Elliot said.

The instructor shook his head. "You'd be dead. Catching that fish was a good move, but you both walked right past all the foods we talked about in training. Come, let's eat."

Elliot and Mandy jumped up eagerly. Their excitement died as the instructor started digging up plants and cutting apart roots. Each time he handed them a handful of leaves, roots, or blossoms, he'd explain again what it was and say, "Eat!"

Elliot and Mandy choked down the odd-tasting mixture of plants. When they finished, the instructor gathered leaves and made hot tea over a fire. The tea actually tasted good. "How do you feel now?" he asked.

Elliot had to admit feeling better.

The instructor knelt and met their eyes. "Every year people die in the wilderness within arm's reach of food. Remember that!" He stood and walked away.

Elliot and Mandy returned to camp. Ms. Lopez and Mr. Boslow waited for them. "Clean up and grab your stuff," Mr. Boslow said. "We're flying back to the Johnson Space Center tonight. Tomorrow's a busy day."

Busy was a gross understatement. The next day started with long classroom sessions followed by a meeting called "Crew Integration." Here for the first time Elliot met the other astronauts from Shuttle Mission STS-97.

The commander, Monte Beaman, had thinning hair and looked like a professor with muscles. He refused to shake their hands. "I think sending a kid into space is a bad publicity stunt," he declared.

The pilot, Victor Lutz, looked more the way Elliot pictured an astronaut. With a square chin and shoulders, and an easygoing manner, Victor always spoke technical jargon like a robot. Elliot figured his first words after being born were probably, "Roger, Mommy, egress complete!"

One payload specialist, RoxeAnn Karch, had bright red hair and freckles that didn't match her serious face. The other payload specialist, Tod Cochran, seemed more relaxed, but Elliot noticed that Tod bit at his lips, squinted, puffed up his cheeks, and wrinkled his forehead when puzzled.

The mission specialist, Shannon Thorpe, had straight blond hair surrounding a thin caring face. She smiled often but her smile disappeared when she worked.

Crew meetings were held more frequently as launch approached. These "timeline reviews" evaluated training and procedures. Mandy and Elliot kept watching stacks of orientation videos on everything from mission control to flight safety. Add to this launch procedures and Shuttle systems, and Elliot's mind threatened to blow a fuse. There were emergency systems, data-processing systems, orbital-maneuvering systems, life-support systems, and bunches of others. The Orbiter orientation manual alone was the size of an encyclopedia. And they were supposed to read it!

Elliot couldn't believe how astronauts went to the bathroom. NASA's technical name for the bathroom was the Waste Control System. In space, both the urinal and toilet used suction to keep the biowaste from floating around. It was like going to the bathroom into a vacuum cleaner. Everyone referred to the urinal tube as Mr. Thirsty. Foot and leg restraints were used to hold astronauts securely in place. Handholds on each side made it easier to line up with the four-inch hole. During practice, Elliot found using the tiny hole *really* tricky.

The instructor told how on earlier flights, a spinning "slinger" was used inside the toilet bowl. It had acted like a garbage disposal, flinging the biowaste against a screen to freeze-dry. On one mission the engineers installed the slinger wrong. After takeoff, when the commander used the Waste Control System, the slinger threw everything back at him. That mission had to use plastic bags.

"Have spacecrafts always had bathrooms?" Elliot asked.

The instructor shook his head. "Alan Shepard didn't have any Waste Control System because his flight was only supposed to last fifteen minutes. He ended up sitting on the launchpad for hours because of delays. He finally told Mission Control he desperately needed to go to the bathroom. After frantic discussions, they gave him permission. It's not something we're proud of," said the instructor, "but NASA's first astronaut went into space with wet pants. That's the reason every astronaut now wears a diaper during launch."

"You mean I have to wear a diaper?" Elliot said loudly.

"All astronauts wear them at launch."

Elliot pointed a warning finger at Mandy. "Don't you dare say anything."

Mandy smiled mischievously.

**THE SECOND DAY** after leaving the engang, Vincent Ole Tome again helped Sambeke at the infirmary. The third day, he helped until the sun was high. Then he told Sambeke, "I must go and be forgiven by my papaa."

Sambeke nodded. "I wish you well, Dreamer Boy."

Vincent's thoughts moved faster than his feet as he left. He dared not go straight to the small-hut of his father. To ask forgiveness, he must first find his mother, Peninah. She would ask an elder to speak to Papaa.

Near the engang, children played. Colorful pegs showed in their pierced ears. Today they played warriors and lions. Some sneaked toward the goat pen like lions trying to attack the herd. The others guarded the pen. Vincent wished his life were still a game.

The sun burned hot above the dried ground. Herders had not yet returned with the weakened herd. Across the valley, a line of women walked a path, carrying large bundles of firewood on their backs. They walked very far to find olive wood from trees that had not yet fallen. Fallen trees near the engang could not be used because already they made a home for the insects.

Inside the engang, Vincent's older sisters visited with girls from a nearby engang. Always the engang had visitors. The group giggled and circled two warriors that also visited. The warriors sat braiding each other's long hair, dyed red with ocher. They pretended not to notice the beautiful girls with their colorful beads and shiny bald heads.

One of the visiting girls was Nasira, someone Vincent enjoyed watching and thinking about. Nasira was beautiful, but not so beautiful she could not think. Vincent wondered if Nasira would ever want to marry someone who was not a warrior. Someone who had been taught at the wood school.

When Vincent found his mother Peninah, she told him, "You must wait until the *engigwana* is finished. They have met to decide the guilt and punishment of a man who stole a cow from your father. Then I will ask the oloiboni to speak to your father about forgiveness."

Vincent waited by the corral. The engigwana was a meeting of elders who judged wrongdoers. Vincent wondered about wrongdoing and about the stories told by the white teacher at the wood school. The teacher said that sometimes white elders killed people for punishment. This Vincent did not understand. In Maasailand, accidents, disease, and wild animals already brought too much death. Each death made the Maasai one person weaker. Why would the white man purposely make themselves weaker?

Here, if one man killed another, he paid the dead man's family forty-nine cattle. This punishment still left the tribe strong. Strength in Maasailand came from life, not death. Was this not true everywhere?

Finally Peninah returned to Vincent. "The engigwana is finished," she said. "Solonga Ole Simel was found guilty of stealing a cow from your father. He must pay Tome five of his best cows."

"That will make Papaa happy," Vincent said.

"Punishment of evil should not make one happy."

Vincent nodded. Peninah called to the oloiboni before he left their engang. The wise and respected elder came to them. His bald head shined with animal fat, and he wore a lion-skin toga that showed his bravery. Creases of wisdom covered his old face. Vincent lowered his head to be touched.

"Oloiboni," Peninah said, "we ask your help. Vincent lost three cows when a lion attacked the herd. For this he has been caned, and now for three days he has been made to leave the engang. Please speak to Tome and ask him to forgive Vincent." From under her toga, Peninah pulled a brightly beaded necklace she had made as a gift for this moment. She held it out to the oloiboni.

Vincent waited patiently, his gaze lowered.

The oloiboni turned to Vincent. "Have you learned from your punishment?"

"Yes, Oloiboni, I have learned," Vincent said, nodding. But his answer was a lie. How could he have learned? He had done no wrong! He had not asked the lion to attack the herd. A spear did not always throw straight. What more could have been done?

"Then come with me," said the oloiboni.

Obediently, Vincent followed Peninah and the proud elder.

"Is Papaa feeling better?" Vincent asked quietly.

Peninah shook her head. "He blames the heat, but something inside his body is not well. He stays in the darkness of his small-hut, sleeping. We bring him food but he eats little. Heat comes to his body, bringing sweat like the dew. Then he shakes with cold. The oloiboni and the paangishu have visited him with their chants and herbs." She shook her head. "Maybe it is Engai's wish."

"Should I ask Sambeke to help Papaa?" Vincent said.

The oloiboni heard Vincent's words and turned with a hard look.

Vincent looked away.

At Tome's small-hut, the oloiboni called out.

Tome answered weakly, "Tijinga," telling the oloiboni to enter. Patiently Vincent waited with his mother. They could hear only mumbled words coming from the small-hut.

Finally the oloiboni returned and spoke. "You are forgiven. Go now and speak to your father."

Vincent nodded his thanks and entered the small-hut. He moved slowly, waiting for his eyes to see. His father lay flat on his skin mat.

"Sit," Tome said weakly.

Vincent rested obediently on the ground.

Today Tome spoke without riddles or proverbs. "This lion you speak of, why did it not attack you?" he asked.

"It did, Papaa. After I threw my spear."

"And why were you not hurt?"

Vincent did not answer.

"I ask you a question," Tome said. "Do you not hear my voice?"

"He did hurt me, Papaa," Vincent said quietly.

"Show me."

Slowly, Vincent rose. Water came to his eyes. Even after forgiveness, Papaa had not believed his words. He turned and showed his back.

Tome allowed a very long silence before he spoke. His voice cracked. "It is good Peninah has cared for your back. Why did she not tell me?"

Vincent pulled his toga back around his shoulders. "She does not know I am hurt."

"Who then has cared for you?"

Reluctantly Vincent said, "Sambeke."

Anger entered Tome's voice. "Why did you not show me you were hurt?"

"Papaa, if truth needs proof, there is no honor."

Tome stared at Vincent through reddened eyes. His gaze and his voice softened. "Honor must be earned. If not, it is like the droppings of the birds."

Vincent stared at the fire without speaking.

"I have forgiven you for the cows you lost. Go now. Again you are my son."

"Yes, Papaa."

As Vincent ducked to leave the small-hut, Tome said, "Vincent, the oloiboni has asked me if you will be part of Embolata Olkiteng. I have told him you will."

Vincent left quickly without answering. His heart hurt worse than his back. In Maasailand, young herders were expected to grow up and become warriors. To become a warrior, Vincent would need to go through many ceremonies and hunt to show his courage. But much was changing in Maasailand. Some parents said the changing world needed men but not warriors. These parents allowed their children to choose between warriorhood and the new ways of the wood school.

One of the ceremonies of warriorhood was Embolata Olkiteng. During Embolata Olkiteng, each boy must catch a young bull by the horns and take it to the ground using only his hands. Doing this proved they were strong and brave.

This ceremony would do two things, Vincent thought. It would take him closer to the final initiation of *emorata* when he would become a man and a warrior. He wished to become a man. But becoming a warrior would take from him his dream. The dream of learning at the wood school.

# CHAPTER TEN

In Houston, Mandy and Elliot started water-survival training. Elliot welcomed getting out of the classroom. For three days they inflated life rafts, exited a mock Orbiter, and practiced survival in water. They even parachuted. A boat pulled them up with a rope and let them go. Mandy was terrified.

Every chance he had, Elliot climbed higher, swam faster, and dived deeper. Mandy couldn't swim very well, so he purposely let her slip from his grip while helping her into the raft. She fell into the water and thrashed about. Making sure the instructor was watching, Elliot reached and pulled her in with a strong hand. He knew what he did was wrong, but he was haunted by the thought of Mandy taking his place. Mandy Harris was *not* going to be the first Junior Astronaut.

After water-survival training, they flew in a big jet called a KC-135. Its hollow insides had been padded.

First they climbed to altitude. Then the jet built up speed and pulled back. Next came pure magic. The jet pushed forward from its steep climb into an arching curve over the top and into a dive. Elliot and Mandy drifted upward, weightlessly bumping about like two balloons.

After thirty seconds, the jet pulled from its dive and climbed again. "We'll float once more for fun," said the instructor. "Then we'll practice eating, drinking, and using equipment."

They practiced until they got queasy. Only later did they learn the KC-135 was nicknamed the Vomit Comet.

The following day they rode in T-38 Talon jet trainers, partly to test for motion sickness. Sitting high up under a bubble canopy and wearing a parachute and helmet, Elliot glanced around wide-eyed as the whining jet taxied onto the runway. He could see only the helmet of the pilot up front. On takeoff, Elliot grinned when the g forces pressed him back in the seat. The T-38 thundered and climbed sharply before finally leveling off.

"Let's take this crate out to the practice range," the pilot's voice crackled inside Elliot's helmet.

"Roger," said Elliot, wishing Mom and Dad could see him right now. They would understand why he didn't want to ranch the rest of his life. His love of flying was something not easily explained with words.

After ten minutes of level flight, the instructor asked through the headset, "Are you ready to rock and roll?"

"I guess," Elliot said.

Instantly, the Talon snapped into a series of head-twisting rolls, followed by stomach-churning dives and loops. Elliot struggled to stay conscious. For the next half hour he had the wildest ride of his entire life.

When the T-38 Talon settled back onto the runway at Ellington Field, Elliot's stomach pushed at his throat. Sweat beaded his forehead. He swallowed hard and waited for the canopy to open so he could get out and breathe fresh air.

Stepping to the ground, the pilot clapped Elliot's back. "So, partner, did you like the yanking and banking?"

"Yeah," Elliot managed weakly. He saw the other T-38 taxi in with Mandy in the back. Climbing out, she looked pale. Stains on her flight suit showed she hadn't been able to keep down her breakfast. Elliot smiled. She probably got some on her white socks. The world's first Junior Astronaut ought to be able to hold down breakfast.

Mandy and Elliot didn't speak much until later that afternoon. Waiting for a lecture, Mandy asked, "Did you get sick on the T-38 flight?"

"Nah, that was nothing."

"I got real sick," she said.

"Maybe you weren't born to be an astronaut."

A hurt expression crossed Mandy's face. Her bottom lip quivered.

A short man with a stiff gait entered the room. "I'm

your instructor for today's talk on astronomy." The man examined them. "So tell me, is man alone in the universe?"

Mandy and Elliot both shrugged.

"Okay, have either of you ever seen UFOs? How about you, young man?" He looked directly at Elliot.

Elliot coughed nervously. "Well, once I woke during the night. Out the window I saw two weird lights way down low in the sky. They were shimmerin' like crazy. They glowed in all kinds of colors: blue, green, orange, and red. They were really close together and bright. They looked like two glowing eyes."

"So, what was it?"

"I woke my parents, and they didn't know, so I called a neighbor who knows a lot about the stars and stuff. He didn't like being woken up. After looking, he said it was just two planets close together in the sky. I felt kind of dumb."

"Well, you weren't so dumb. What you saw was a conjunction of planets. That can be very impressive. Seldom do bright planets come together so closely in the sky. To the ancients, a conjunction was a mystical sign of great events about to happen on Earth. The colors you saw came from light refracting as it passed through the thick atmosphere of Earth—like a prism."

The instructor looked at Mandy. "How about you, young lady? Have you ever seen a UFO?"

Mandy smiled. "No, but we made one once."

"How so?"

"We took birthday candles, straws, and a plastic dry-cleaning bag. We built a small hot-air balloon and let it go at night. It climbed up real high with an eerie, wavering glow. Lots of people around the city saw it and called the police. They sent up a police helicopter. It was in the newspaper's police report the next day. We never told anyone."

The instructor smiled. "So, we do have two curious minds here." He walked over and picked up a small telescope. "Do you know what this is?"

"A telescope," Elliot blurted, glad to be the first to answer at least one question.

"No," said the instructor. "It's a time machine."

"No way," Elliot said.

The instructor smiled. "This doesn't show you what's in the sky. It shows you what *was* in the sky years ago. Some stars don't even exist anymore—we see only the light they sent out hundreds, thousands, sometimes millions of years ago." He pointed up. "The ancients thought stars were mystical lights on a dome. We know that's not true. But do we know what *is* true? The cosmos is more fantastic than we can ever imagine." The instructor adjusted his glasses and bent down as if telling a secret. "Imagine this!"

Elliot and Mandy leaned forward.

"If the Sun were the size of a basketball, the Earth would be a pea a hundred feet away. Jupiter would be a Ping-Pong ball five hundred feet away. Pluto, a pinhead nearly a mile away. And beyond that, vast nothingness.

"If you traveled as fast as light, 670 million miles per hour, it would take four years to get to the nearest star, Alpha Centauri." The instructor held up the telescope. "When you see Alpha Centauri, you see only how it looked four years ago. That star and perhaps as many as a hundred billion others make up our rather small spiral galaxy called the Milky Way. Planet Earth floats way out in one of the less significant spiral arms.

"Okay, get ready!" he said suddenly. "Now the fun really starts. Travel with me!"

Elliot took a deep breath.

"Beyond our galaxy we get into intergalactic space. The nearest major galaxy is Andromeda. Light we see from Andromeda left there two million years ago. Can you imagine—two million light-years away?"

The instructor walked around in front of his desk. His voice grew more excited. "Beyond Andromeda there are clouds of other galaxies, billions and billions of them, farther away than we can even imagine. And this only scratches the surface of the universe. We're talking big-time BIG!"

Sweat gleamed on his forehead as he pointed skyward. "Out there are quasars, black holes, secrets of the cosmos, secrets to our origin, secrets to our destiny."

Mandy twisted at her pen. Elliot found himself breathing fast.

"You are *both* part of that search for secrets," said the instructor.

Elliot glanced over at Mandy. Again the feeling

94

came to him he could not fight. *He* was the one going into space. Not her.

**VINCENT FELT AS** if he lived in two worlds. Each day he herded, hunted, and lived the life forced on him by his father, Tome. Every word, every step, every ceremony, brought him closer to the final initiation of emorata when he would become a man and a warrior.

Each evening he entered another world at the infirmary with Sambeke. There he learned to read and he learned numbers. He learned of things other than the cattle, lions, hunting, and warriorhood. Sambeke showed him maps of strange places at the top and bottom of the world where water froze and all the ground was covered by snow and ice. Sambeke had pictures of a great white animal called a polar bear, an animal more dangerous than a lion. Sambeke also spoke of places where people made wide paths that carried millions of cars.

"Could there really be so many cars?" Vincent asked.

Sambeke nodded. "Yes, enough to make the sky dirty."

This Vincent could not believe. He had seen only the few cars the white man drove when they came to the engang. They came bringing their own god and saying the Maasai god, Engai, was not real. For this reason Vincent did not trust the white man. Engai had made the Maasai. This was something the Maasai had known for all time. The words of the ancients were the words of truth. If the Maasai were real, and all the world was real, then Engai, the maker of all, must also be real. This Vincent understood. But some things Vincent did not understand. He did not know why the Maasai killed to show courage.

Each day, the other boys, led by Leboo, taunted Vincent for not killing a lion. Vincent knew it was a person's heart that threw a spear and not his arm. For this reason, Vincent carried his spear low. The boys shoved him. "You carry your spear with a broken arm!" they shouted, poking and tripping him.

Once Vincent fought the boys, and they held him down and tortured him like a cheetah holding a squealing rabbit. So Vincent walked alone, and with him walked the fear of the ceremony Embolata Olkiteng. On that day, with all the other boys watching, he would have to take a large bullock to the ground with his hands. This would prove his strength and courage.

But could he?

Finally the day came that brought that answer.

Vincent awoke early. Because Papaa was sick, another elder joined Vincent for the long walk to the engang that held the ceremony Embolata Olkiteng. Other boys had gathered, including Leboo.

Leboo spoke loudly, bragging of the buffalo, rhinoceroses, elephants, and lions he had killed. "The bullock will not dare come into the corral when he sees me!" he bragged.

"That will be because he has already run from me," said the boy Tinga.

"I could take down two at once," shouted another.

Vincent watched silently as an elder gathered the boys together. First the elder spoke to them of bravery and of honor. Then he tapped their heads with his walking stick in the order they would face the bullocks. Vincent was tapped last.

One by one, the boys entered the corral. Alone, with the others watching, each boy chased a fresh bullock in circles, waving and whistling. When finally they caught the wild-eyed animal, they struggled to bring it to the ground. Some lifted at the legs. Others pushed at the body. Each boy had to stay in the corral until their bullock no longer stood.

Some young bulls had grown larger than others. When it was Vincent's turn, his worst fear became real. A bullock larger than any other was let into the corral. Fear pushed on Vincent's chest like a heavy stone.

The other boys jeered and clapped. "You cannot move his ear!" shouted Leboo.

Vincent tried to swallow but could not.

# CHAPTER ELEVEN

**E**ach week in Houston became more mind-boggling. During orientation to the Orbiter simulator, Elliot stared in numbed disbelief at the hundreds and hundreds of switches, circuit breakers, toggles, instruments, screens, warning lights, and other controls that covered the flight deck. Not just the front dash, but both side walls, the whole ceiling, and even behind the seats. This made the Cessna 150 that he took flight lessons with seem like a kid's tricycle.

Classes were given in Orbiter maintenance. Everything needed to be kept spotlessly clean. After vacuuming, Mandy and Elliot practiced wiping down the walls of the mock-up Orbiter. Elliot wished his mom could see him cleaning and being neat like this. His bedroom back at the ranch would definitely not cut it in space.

As part of mission training, Elliot and Mandy practiced heating food in the galley and serving it on trays.

Orbiters did not have a refrigerator, so dehydrated food packages were slid into a dispenser where a huge needle squirted in water. Velcro straps kept food trays from floating around.

After eating, they wiped trays and utensils and packed up garbage. With no showers on the Orbiter, Elliot and Mandy practiced keeping themselves clean with washcloths. Brushing teeth was the same as usual except they had to spit into a washcloth or swallow.

For the first time, Elliot started training and practicing with the SAREX—the Shuttle Amateur Radio Experiment. In orbit, he would talk to dozens of people around the world. He looked forward to this part of the mission.

More practice time was spent in the KC-135 Vomit Comet. These flights let them try washing hands, brushing teeth, moving around, and serving up food while floating. Elliot liked not having to eat gooey food from squeeze tubes like earlier astronauts. It was tricky, though, bringing food to his mouth. Once, he bumped Mandy while she was eating spaghetti and meatballs. It made a real mess. Another time, a bite got away from Elliot. Instead of reaching his fork to bring it back, he launched himself after it, catching it with his mouth. Mandy laughed.

Most nights Elliot called home. He missed his parents and the ranch terribly. People in Montana spoke normally. Here they spoke "tech talk" like robots, with words like *ingress, egress, nominal, acquisition, request, confirm, status, advise, stow, negative, abort, stabilize, deploy,* and *uplink.* Elliot longed for a simple conversation, like, "Do you think it will rain tomorrow?" "Yup, I reckon."

More and more, Elliot resented Mandy Harris. As a person she was okay, but she was such a brain she made him feel stupid. Each day she got more and more attention. At night Elliot lay in bed, sure he was going to be replaced. He knew he was being a jerk, but the only way he knew how to handle his feelings was to try to make Mandy look bad.

Training continued with practice fighting onboard fires. They also practiced aborted missions at takeoff, shortly after takeoff, partway into space, or in orbit.

Their next weeks of training took place at the Kennedy Space Center, home of the mosquito. In case of fire on the pad, they learned how to ride a big basket on rollers down a cable away from the tower. On the ground they practiced jumping into a tanklike escape carrier. Riding in the tank was fun, but Elliot had never had so many mosquito bites.

"If the tower fire doesn't kill you," joked the instructor, "the mosquitoes will finish you off when you reach the ground."

That's no joke, thought Elliot.

In case of problems right after takeoff, they practiced sliding down a simulated pole. This would clear them from the Orbiter to open their parachutes.

The following week, Elliot and Mandy took high-altitude physiological training. While waiting for the instructor, Mandy asked Elliot, "Why do you hate me?"

Elliot laughed. "I don't hate you."

"Then why do you always try to make me look bad?"

Elliot thought a while. "No girl with silly white socks is going to take my place in space."

"I'm not trying to take your place!" Mandy almost shouted. "Can't you see, I'm here in case you get sick or hurt. I'm not *trying* to take your place!"

"Then how come you show me up all the time?"

"I'm just trying to do my best, the same as you. You were better at wilderness and water survival. And you were better at parachuting and launch-tower aborts. You've been better at lots of things. But it doesn't matter because we're a team."

Elliot didn't answer. He wanted to go into space more than he wanted to breathe air. He knew the things he said to Mandy were wrong, but he didn't know what else he could do to make sure that he was the first Junior Astronaut in space.

At that moment the instructor entered the room and motioned them back to the chamber facilities. "Okay, listen up," he said. "The altitude chamber will let you discover how each of you reacts to different kinds of stress and lack of oxygen. In the case of Orbiter decompression, you must recognize personal symptoms of oxygen starvation. First, let's learn how the human body works."

After three hours of lecturing, Mandy and Elliot entered the altitude chamber. It was like a big air tank.

"Sit down," said the instructor. "I've given you each a list of symptoms you might experience before passing out. As pressure is lowered, your individual symptoms could be ringing in the ears, skin tingling, numbness, fingers feeling swollen, tunnel vision, or whatever. You need to learn how your body reacts to these extreme conditions." He gave thumbs-up to the technician outside the chamber. "Okay, let's go up," he said.

At a simulated fourteen thousand feet, Elliot found that things looked funny. He had tunnel vision. Mandy said her arms felt numb.

"Good," said the instructor. "Now we'll wear oxygen masks and go up higher." He gave them each ten differently shaped blocks. "When I tell you, take off your mask and insert these blocks into the panel in front of you."

Slowly, the air pressure in the tank was lowered to simulate the thin air at twenty thousand feet. "Okay," said the instructor, "take off your masks and insert all the blocks in their correct holes." He spoke firmly. "Remember, when you notice a symptom, put your mask back on immediately."

The blocks seemed simple to Elliot until the fourth one. Then he struggled and twisted and pushed, but it wouldn't go in. His vision started fuzzing out around the edges as if he were looking down a tube. Quickly he pulled his mask back on and took deep breaths. Beside him, Mandy had finished seven of her blocks before putting on her mask. Elliot kicked the bench.

When the tank was flooded with air again, they removed their masks. "She beat you on that one," chided the instructor.

Elliot and Mandy glanced at each other.

Next the instructor gave them notepads. "Now," he said, "write down your name, address, age, and birthday."

When they finished, the instructor looked at their pads. "Very good," he said. "Now, put on your masks and turn to a new page. We'll drop the pressure to simulate twenty thousand feet again."

As they waited, Elliot noticed that the instructor was watching the chamber technician outside the window. Before the instructor turned back, Elliot scribbled down his name and address. Through his oxygen mask he saw Mandy watching. Her eyes looked like alien bug eyes through her mask. He glared back at her until she looked away. Elliot kept his pad faced downward on his lap.

The instructor turned and motioned. "Okay," he said, his voice muffled by his oxygen mask. "Take off your masks and write your name, address, age, and birthday, again."

Elliot breathed deeply and removed his mask. Keeping his pad tilted, he pretended to write fast. All he really had to finish writing was his age and birthday. He wrote down fourteen. Now his birthday. That was August, or was it November? He squeezed the pen harder—this was crazy. His birthday was August 15. He struggled to write but couldn't. The black tunnel clouded at his vision. He shook his head. He wasn't putting on his mask until he finished. No girl was going to beat him.

Elliot felt Mandy trying to put on his mask for him. He shoved her away. Then the instructor's strong hands forced his mask on firmly.

After a couple of breaths, Elliot said strongly, "I was going to put it on!"

"You were going to die!" snapped the instructor. "Look at your pad of paper."

Elliot looked down. He had written his age clearly. But the August started out with a big *A* and *U*, then the writing flattened out and drifted off the page. He glanced over at Mandy's page. She had finished her name and part of her address before her writing became sloppy and she put on her own mask.

"You started out well," said the instructor to Elliot. "Seldom does anyone even finish their address. But you didn't know when to quit. What were you trying to do? Beat her?" He motioned toward Mandy. "You wouldn't even let her help you. In this business everybody's on the same team. Pulling a stunt like that in space could kill the whole crew and destroy a mission." He jotted a note on his notepad. "Okay, you're finished here."

I'm probably finished, period, Elliot thought.

**IN THE CORRAL** at the ceremony Embolata Olkiteng, Vincent stood alone facing his bullock. All the other boys watched. This big young bull had horns like knives and dull eyes that glared like a Cape buffalo.

"Do you want me to help you?" yelled Leboo. "You cannot lift the bullock's dung!"

Vincent eased forward, holding out his hand. The young bull turned nervously. Vincent stopped. Each animal today had entered the corral weak with hunger, but fear had given them strength. Vincent dared not frighten his bullock. Slowly he moved forward again. When he could lay his hand on the animal's back, he gently stroked the big body, moving closer to its head. He knew that a bullock's body must turn with the head. If its nose was pulled to the sky, it would fall.

Leboo yelled, "He's going to kiss the bull!"

Vincent ran his right arm gently over the bullock's neck until he could reach the nose. He had only one chance. If the bullock escaped, it would become strong again with fear. Leboo kept shouting and taunting.

Vincent stroked the bull carefully. When he could feel the warm air coming from the nostrils, he drew in a deep breath. It was time! Without warning, Vincent dropped all his weight onto the bullock's neck. At the same time he gripped and twisted the nose with both hands.

The bull jerked hard, but Vincent pulled with all his strength. He braced both feet. Slowly, the big nose bent backward over the animal's shoulder toward the sky. Vincent strained, wedging his elbow behind a horn. Like a huge boulder beside a cliff, the bullock rocked back and forth, balancing. Then his body crashed to the dusty ground. Pinned under the big head, Vincent held to the horn and nose so the struggling bull could not stand again.

When the bullock finally relaxed, Vincent loosened his grip and slid free. He gave the young bull a push. It scrambled up and charged away. Vincent returned and sat beside the other boys.

"You fight your bull like a coward!" hissed Leboo, his voice sharp with anger.

An elder held up his hand for silence. Then he spoke. "Today all of you have showed your bravery. You have done this with the strength of your bodies. Vincent has taken the largest bullock to the ground with the strength of his body, and also with the strength of his head."

The elder looked straight at Leboo. "Remember this. The bravest warrior is *not* the one with the strongest body, but the one with the strongest mind. Today Vincent has proved himself the strongest among you." The elder nodded to Vincent with respect.

Vincent's mouth could not speak. He looked at those gathered. Slowly each boy nodded their respect— all except Leboo. Anger and hatred burned in his eyes. Vincent knew he would face Leboo's anger again.

The ceremony Embolata Olkiteng brought changes to Vincent's life. After taking down the largest bullock with his hands, the elders had called him the bravest. Now for the first time, other boys asked to hear Vincent's thoughts. They asked also if he would join their hunts. This angered Leboo who still thought himself the bravest and strongest.

Vincent avoided Leboo. But Leboo's anger was like wind that blows where it is not wanted. One evening, while visiting another engang, Vincent stood watching his favorite girl, Nasira. She threaded beads with the other girls.

Leboo approached and called out loudly, "Vincent! I challenge you to a contest."

"What contest?" Vincent asked.

All the girls, including Nasira, turned to watch.

"Tomorrow, you and I will each hunt. If you are as brave as the elders say, then you will kill a lion."

Vincent spoke carefully. "What if I do not wish to hunt for lion?"

Letting his voice growl with anger, Leboo said, "Then all the girls will know you are a coward! An earless dog!"

Vincent saw the girls watching, and he saw Nasira's curious face. Her smooth head shined beautifully like the moon. He could not swallow his words. Strongly, Vincent said, "I will hunt lion! Tomorrow, when the sun leaves the sky, we will know who is the bravest."

"You will be lucky to bring back a rabbit," Leboo scoffed, laughing loudly.

Anger pulled at Vincent's lips. "My spear will hunt for me. Not my mouth."

The girls giggled. Leboo looked struck. Hatred chased the laughter from his mouth as he walked away.

# CHAPTER TWELVE

Elliot wanted to go into space more than anything in the whole world, but during chamber
training, he had crossed the line and cheated.
He knew it, and Mandy knew it. They did not speak all
afternoon. Instead of exercising that night in the gym,
Elliot sat alone in his room, angry at the world and
angry at himself.

Why had he been so selfish? Mandy hadn't done
anything wrong—nobody could blame her for being
here and doing her best. Elliot couldn't stop the big
tears that swelled into his eyes. Tonight, he didn't dare
call his mom and dad. They would be so disappointed
if they knew what kind of son they had raised.

"Mom and Dad didn't raise a cheater," he said
loudly. "I'm such a jerk!" Deliberately he picked up the
phone and called Mr. Boslow. "Can you get Ms. Lopez
and Mandy and meet me here at crew quarters?" he
asked.

"Why?" said Mr. Boslow.

"Please," Elliot said. "It's important."

Half an hour later, a car pulled to a stop out front. Elliot greeted everyone at the door.

"What's up, sport?" Mr. Boslow asked, as he and Ms. Lopez entered. Mandy followed quietly behind.

Elliot tried to keep his voice steady. "Uh, I have something to say—why don't you all sit down." With everyone seated around the table, Elliot looked at Mandy. Hesitantly he spoke. "I'm sorry. I've been a real jerk, trying to make you look bad."

Mandy looked down. "It's no big deal," she mumbled.

"Yeah, it is." Elliot glanced over at Mr. Boslow and Ms. Lopez. Their faces showed little expression. "Mandy is the one who should go into space. She's the smartest, and she doesn't cheat."

"Cheat?" Ms. Lopez said, looking puzzled.

"Yeah. I cheated during chamber training. Then I didn't let Mandy help me put my oxygen mask back on. All I cared about was me."

"So, what are you suggesting?" Mr. Boslow asked.

"Mandy should go up instead of me. I'll do everything I can to help her do a good job."

Mr. Boslow and Ms. Lopez gave each other strange looks. "We're not the ones to decide," Ms. Lopez said. "But we'll be talking to the review board tomorrow. Whatever happens, you did the right thing being honest."

Elliot felt better, but he still had to square things with Mandy. "Are you mad at me?" he asked her.

She didn't answer right away. When she did, the

smile was missing from her freckled face. "Yeah."

"It's okay if you are," Elliot said.

"What do you have against girls, anyway?"

"Maybe I'm afraid you might be better than me."

"And what if I was? Then what?"

Elliot scuffed his shoe on the smooth floor. "I guess it's no big deal," he said in a quiet voice.

Mandy stood. "That's right, it's no big deal. We're a team—that's all that matters." Suddenly she hugged Elliot.

Elliot hugged her back. "A good team," he answered. "If I haven't screwed things up too bad."

The next day, Elliot and Mandy were taken over to a neutral-buoyancy water tank called the Weightless Environment Training Facility (WETF). Because the first Junior Astronaut would not make a space walk, the WETF was not part of the official training.

For the first time Mandy's thick white socks didn't bother Elliot. He tried to help her with everything to make up for the last five months. After two hours of classroom training to learn about scuba diving, they suited up and dove with tanks. It was a blast floating and gliding around underwater. Everybody looked strange with masks on and regulators in their mouths.

After a small lunch, they returned to the tank. This time they wore actual space suits modified for underwater use. The suits were too heavy to stand in. Assistant divers held the air tubes and helped Elliot and Mandy submerge. They worked their way down a ladder into a mock-up bay of a Shuttle Orbiter.

Weight was adjusted so they neither floated nor sank. Neutrally buoyant, they just hung weightless in the shimmering water. Helmet communications let them talk.

"How are you doing?" Elliot asked Mandy.

Mandy's voice came back a bit garbled. "Great! Isn't this wild?"

"It's fantastic!"

Slowly they moved, hand over hand along the Orbiter bay. One of the assistant divers motioned for Elliot to push away from the sides. Elliot did and immediately wished he hadn't. With nothing to grasp, he floundered helplessly. When he kicked his legs and grabbed for the Orbiter bay, his body rolled sideways, then upside down.

"Here, I'll help you," Mandy said.

"I can't even see you," Elliot said.

"Put your right hand backward and grab my leg."

Elliot did as she said. Carefully, he rotated himself upright. "Thanks a bunch," he said, grabbing a handhold.

That afternoon after neutral-buoyancy training ended, Ms. Lopez drove Elliot and Mandy back to crew quarters. "Well, Elliot," she said, as she drove. "The astronaut review board met today. They feel you'll do just fine as the first Junior Astronaut."

Elliot stammered with surprise. "I, uh, but how could they?"

"They aren't looking for superhumans or computer brains. What they want is somebody who is honest, tries hard, and works as part of a team. To be honest, the board had all but decided to replace you because of your attitude. But after hearing what happened last night, the board agreed you will do fine. Mandy will continue as the alternate selection, and we will all work toward the mission of launching the first Junior Astronaut into space."

"I promise I'll do my best," Elliot said. "I'll work as a team."

Sitting together in the backseat, Mandy poked him in the ribs. "You better," she whispered. "Or I'll stuff my white socks in your mouth while you're asleep."

Five months had passed at the Johnson Space Center. More and more, everybody talked about the mission. The astronauts of STS-97 met for their first launch readiness review.

By now, the crew were fast becoming friends. The only person who remained distant was Commander Beaman. He seemed all right with everybody else, but with Elliot and Mandy he barked orders impatiently during training.

One day, Elliot asked Commander Beaman, "Am I doing okay?"

"As well as can be expected," Commander Beaman said gruffly. "Children shouldn't be going into space." Before Elliot could answer, the commander walked away.

Frustrated, Elliot returned to training with Mandy.

That afternoon, Ms. Lopez met them. "Well," she said, "are you two ready for a change?"

"Sure!" they exclaimed.

"Good. Tomorrow you fly to Ames Research Center in California to begin medical experiments."

"You mean where they use needles?" Elliot asked weakly.

She nodded devilishly. "Yeah, tons of needles!"

Elliot and Mandy gave each other grim looks.

**AFTER TELLING LEBOO** he would hunt for lion, Vincent walked quickly across the valley to the infirmary.

Sambeke met him at the door. "Dreamer Boy, have you come early to talk to strangers on the radio?"

Vincent shook his head. At this moment, a stranger's voice on the black box would bring no magic. Quietly, he admitted what he had done.

Disappointment flickered in Sambeke's eyes. "I have told you, Dreamer Boy, the laws of Kenya say it is wrong to kill a lion."

"Papaa says there is only the law of the Maasai."

Sambeke shook his head slowly. "Anger makes you brave, but it does not let you think."

"But Leboo has called me a coward in front of the girls." Vincent did not tell of his favorite girl, Nasira.

Sambeke spoke more softly. "Courage does not use anger to kill. When you are angry at Leboo, you are his prisoner. He controls you."

"Leboo does not control me!"

"Yes he does! You have given Leboo strength by accepting his challenge. Tell me, is the moon a coward if you challenge it to fall from the sky and it does not fall?" Again Sambeke shook his head. "That is not what makes a coward. A coward is the hyena that growls with a tail between its legs."

"I am not a hyena!" Vincent said. "I am brave. I can kill a lion!"

Sambeke nodded. "You are brave, or you would not come here. But killing a lion will prove only that you are foolish. It will prove Leboo controls you."

"I thought you were my friend!" Vincent shouted.

"Follow your heart, not your anger. What has happened to Dreamer Boy? Today I speak with someone who runs from his shadow."

Vincent turned and ran out the door toward the engang.

Sambeke called after him, "Vincent, come back!"

Vincent kept running. He was tired of being called a coward. When he followed his heart, people laughed. No longer would they laugh. No longer would Papaa carry shame for the ways of his son.

At the engang, Vincent went to his father's small-hut. When Tome had given him permission, he entered. "Papaa," Vincent announced, "Tomorrow I will kill a lion!"

Lying on his back, his breaths ragged, Tome nodded. "Are you clever?" he whispered.

Vincent nodded. "Yes, Papaa."

"How clever?"

"As clever as a mongoose."

Tome forced his words. "What is the greediest thing on earth?"

"A fire, Papaa."

Tome nodded gravely, his eyes curious. "Engai does not listen to the snake," he said. "So tell me, what has made my son so brave?"

Vincent shrugged. "It is the way of the Maasai."

Tome nodded, a smile creasing his dry lips. He let his eyes close.

When Tome did not open his eyes or speak again, Vincent left the small-hut. The black sky had filled with stars. Vincent sat alone near the corral. He kept the tears of a coward from his eyes. An engang dog came near, and Vincent threw a stone hard. The dog yelped and ran. Tonight, Vincent wanted no friends. Carefully he sharpened his spear until it would cut his fingernail. This done, he entered the small-hut and slept.

While he slept, dreams came. Vincent dreamed he had killed the biggest lion in all of Maasailand. With the lion's ears and tail held high on his spear, he returned to the engang. In the dream, girls stood beside his path. They reached out to touch his toga, especially the girl Nasira. Leboo hid in the shadows of a small-hut, a rabbit in his hand.

Before the sun's first light, Vincent's dreams left him and he awoke. Moving quietly, he made ready for the hunt. He ate meat left from last night's meal, and he filled his calabash with milk. Two of his younger brothers sat in the corral, watching the herd. Vincent nodded to them silently and left the engang.

Spear in hand, Vincent moved across the flat countryside toward the shadowed mountains where he had seen lions come for water. He let his thoughts keep alive his anger, like wood added to a fire. Without anger, he could not kill a lion. It helped to throw rocks. Today, even the small dik-dik ran from him.

When Vincent stopped to eat, he chased two hyenas from the shade of an umbrella tree. The hyenas circled, their ugly heads held low. He threw more rocks at them. After eating, Vincent kept walking. The hyenas returned to their shade.

When the sun had floated high in the sky, a small pond appeared. Vincent crept close and hid behind a bush. Waiting, he watched waterbuck, wildebeests, zebras, and even two giraffes come to drink. This was a good place. Later, the lions would come for water.

Vincent did not have to wait long.

A deep chilling growl scattered a pack of baboons near the pond. Their screams and grunting barks hung in the still air. Alone, a large female lion appeared from the brush and angled toward the pond.

Vincent crouched and gripped his spear. Now he would kill a lion. He would prove he was no coward.

# CHAPTER THIRTEEN

**M**edical experiments began at Ames Research Center in California. Elliot knew he was in trouble when the first doctor he met started out by saying, "Our studies will evaluate virtually all of your body systems, including musculoskeletal, neuro-vestibular, cardiovascular, and cardiopulmonary. Studies on your regulatory physiology will include fluid-electrolyte, endocrinology, and hematology. You can expect to—"

"Excuse me," Elliot interrupted.

"Yes, what is it?"

"Are you going to give us shots?"

The doctor looked as if he had been short-circuited. He stood for a full five seconds with his glasses hung low on his nose and his mouth open. Then he said, "Yes, there will be a certain number of injections. More significant will be the fluids such as blood drawn from your body."

"Blood . . . with needles?" Elliot asked, cringing.

"Is that a problem?"

Mandy spoke up. "He loves shots, Doctor. That's his favorite part of training."

"It is not!" Elliot said, jabbing Mandy with his elbow.

"They're going to take *blood* from our *bodies*," Mandy said diabolically.

"Can we continue?" the doctor asked.

"Yes," Elliot muttered. Already he could feel huge needles sucking blood from his body until he was empty as a flat inner tube.

As the doctor kept talking, Mandy whispered, "Shots don't hurt as bad if you wear white socks."

Elliot chuckled and settled into his seat.

Elliot understood about one-tenth of this lecture. He did gather that for millions of years the human body had evolved with gravity. In space, everything changed. Balance, touch, taste, muscles, red-blood-cell count, everything was affected. A heart changed sizes. The spine straightened, making you taller. Fluids bunched up in the head and chest. Muscles shriveled up. Bones got smaller.

"How can bones get smaller?" Elliot asked. "Where do they go to?"

"The calcium is excreted with your urine," the doctor said.

"Great," muttered Elliot.

"Just don't go to the bathroom," Mandy teased.

Elliot nudged Mandy. "Shut up."

"By the time you go into space," said the doctor, "we'll know every system of your body better than you know your name. We'll know your metabolism, chemistry, exact blood volume, everything. Consider yourself a human guinea pig."

"Squeeeeeeeee," squealed Elliot.

The doctor failed to smile, but Mandy cracked up.

Elliot hated going to doctors. Now, for two weeks, he and Mandy went full-time. They were poked, jabbed, pricked, X-rayed, inspected, questioned, observed, and tested. They ran on treadmills. With tubes in their mouths and clips on their noses, they ran until they were out of breath. The tube was hard to breathe through. Spit kept running down their chins.

Another test, the magnetic resonance imaging, was right out of *Star Trek*. They lay motionless on a table while their bodies moved through a buzzing white cylinder.

Finally Elliot and Mandy finished at Ames, and they headed back to the Johnson Space Center. "I can't believe we have to come back here for more tests," Mandy said.

"We do?" said Elliot.

"Yup, at launch minus six weeks."

Elliot gave Mandy a sick look. The thought of more shots and blood tests made him want to go home. He'd give anything to be working his way across a sagebrush-covered hill on his horse, Cooper, right now.

Before landing at Ellington Field, Mr. Boslow came

back and knelt beside their seats. "We have a little surprise for you two when we arrive."

Elliot and Mandy squirmed with excitement as they touched down and pulled to a stop. Halfway down the steps, Elliot spotted the surprise. "Mom! Dad!" he shouted, breaking into a run. Elliot hugged his parents hard. "Man, am I glad to see you guys!"

Beside Mr. and Mrs. Schroeder stood Mandy's parents. Mandy, too, screamed and ran forward.

Mr. Boslow and Ms. Lopez walked up smiling. "Tomorrow, you two may take the day off," they announced. "No shots, no blood tests, no lectures, no nothing!"

"Whoooeeee!" Elliot hollered.

"Yippeeeeee!" Mandy jumped up and down.

"So, I hear it's been a big vacation," Dalton joked.

Elliot held up his arms to show the black-and-blue marks from all the blood tests. "A real picnic!" he said. "I've worked harder here than I ever worked on the ranch."

"That's not saying much," Dalton said.

Angie gave Dalton a sharp glance.

Ms. Lopez pointed. "This way." Laughing and all talking at once, everybody loaded into the van.

That night, after visiting late, Elliot's parents slept at crew quarters. Words couldn't describe all that had happened in the last six months, but Elliot tried. He asked questions about the ranch, but Dalton didn't say much except that it had been real dry.

The next day they toured the base. Elliot and Mandy introduced their parents to tons of people. Dalton and Angie delivered a huge card signed by Elliot's teachers and schoolmates. Each had written a small message.

"They'd freak if they knew all I've done!" said Elliot.

His parents agreed.

Everyone stayed a second night before leaving. At seven-thirty the next morning, Mr. Boslow stopped to pick up Elliot and Mandy for a day of classes called Mission Profile. "We have to get going," he said.

Elliot and Mandy hugged and hugged their parents good-bye, then reluctantly climbed into the waiting van. They waved one last time. Elliot shouted out the window, "Mom! Dad! I'll see you at launch!"

Elliot's mom wiped at her eyes as she waved back.

**VINCENT OLE TOME** crouched near the pond and watched the lion. Each time she lowered her head to drink, he moved forward, gripping his spear hard. Thoughts screamed inside his head like a pack of wild baboons. Why was he hunting this lion? Was anger making him foolish?

Vincent ignored the questions. It didn't matter now. The lion's tail twitched. Her huge chest moved with each breath. Vincent thanked the breeze for blowing his smells away from the water. He crept forward, heart pounding. This was the moment. When the lion lowered her head again, he would run in. As she turned, he would throw his spear hard and straight.

Slowly, the lion lowered her great whiskered mouth back to the water. Vincent raised his spear and held his breath. He had only one throw. One chance.

A scratching sound came from the shrubs to Vincent's side. Two young lion cubs ran out from the brush. They chased each other, tumbling and spinning. At the pond's edge they bumped against the legs of their mother, then drank from the pond. The lion stood patiently. When the cubs finished drinking, they played with their mother's twitching tail.

Slowly, Vincent lowered his spear and smiled. Many times he had watched cubs play. Watching the cubs made the anger empty from his body. He could not leave cubs without a mother. Sambeke was right. Killing a lion would not prove bravery. It would only take another breath of life from Maasailand. Today the lions had not hurt the cattle, so today he would not hurt the lions. Engai could not want such death.

Another sound from the brush made Vincent more glad he had not killed the lion. Four female lions walked toward the pond. Following behind them came a large male, his shaggy mane swinging from side to side as he walked. Vincent backed carefully away. His spear was of no use now.

In the direction of home, the sun fell slowly toward the ground. Vincent knew he must race the darkness to the engang. If he were late, he would have to make a fire and spend the night alone with the eyes of lions and hyenas gleaming in the night. This was not his wish. Purposely, he let the ground move fast under his sandals. He held his spear ready on his shoulder.

When at last the engang appeared, the night had pushed all the light from the sky. Vincent allowed a thankful breath to escape his mouth. Tonight, anger did not hold his thoughts. He could face Leboo now, even with the girls watching. Loudly, he called to his brother, Ketere, who guarded the corral.

The young boy ran over. "You are alive! You are alive!"

"Why would I not be alive?" asked Vincent sharply, pulling branches from the gate to enter.

"Go speak with Peninah," said Ketere. "Something very bad has happened!"

"What?" asked Vincent.

Ketere did not answer.

Vincent ran to the small-hut of his mother Peninah. "Mamaa," he called.

Peninah met him and took his arm. "You are safe!"

"Why would I not be safe?" Vincent asked.

"Have you not been told?"

"Only that something very bad has happened. Has something happened to Papaa?"

Peninah gripped his arm harder. "It is Leboo. He was attacked by the lions."

"Where is he? Does he still live?" Vincent asked.

"Warriors found him. He still breathes, so they have brought him here." Peninah pointed to her hut. "Herbs and chants have not helped, so now the oloiboni has left Leboo to die. Nothing more can be done."

"Can I see him?" Vincent asked.

Peninah nodded and ducked inside. Vincent followed through the small opening. Inside, the smell of herbs and death mixed with the olive-wood smoke. Vincent coughed. He squinted and saw Leboo's body lying still beside the fire. Blood covered the goatskins and the ground. Vincent stared hard. Was this the loud and boastful Leboo who had challenged him to kill a lion?

"Have you sent for Sambeke?" Vincent asked.

"The oloiboni has done all that can be done," Peninah said.

"No!" Vincent said. "Sambeke can help!" He crouched over Leboo and listened for his breath. Touching his neck as Sambeke had taught him, Vincent felt for the beating of Leboo's heart. He felt long before sitting upright. Softly, but deliberately, he spoke. "Mamaa—Leboo is dead!"

# CHAPTER FOURTEEN

Visiting with his parents lifted Elliot's spirits. Now, with launch only ten weeks away, he needed to get his head "in the game." Training held a sense of urgency. The crew met more often, simulating countdown and launch.

They watched more videos, including one on systems malfunctions that showed the Shuttle *Challenger* blowing up. Mandy and Elliot looked quietly at each other. Neither said anything, but the exploding fireball left a knot in Elliot's stomach. The image burned into his thoughts.

This mission, called Return to Planet Earth, was part of the larger ATLAS (Atmospheric Laboratory for Applications and Science) program, which was in turn part of NASA's Mission to Planet Earth. The mission would help study Earth and its environment. One responsibility of the first Junior Astronaut was to conduct live interviews with networks of connected schools.

Sounding stupid in front of a million students wasn't Elliot's idea of a good time.

Training continued. Some classes were sobering. Elliot never realized that the atmosphere was like a superthin eggshell wrapped around the world. In fact, if the Earth were the size of a basketball, the atmosphere would be as thin as a fingernail. That thin shell was all that protected the world from outer space.

Even scarier were all the things affecting this thin fingernail of air. Gases and ash spewed out of volcanoes. Dust and ash collected from the burning of forests. Farmers used tons of chemicals. Pollution poured out of factories and automobiles.

Effects on the atmosphere from space were harder for Elliot to understand. It made sense to him that the atmosphere acted like a big window that held in heat, causing a greenhouse effect. But things like solar activity, magnetic storms, ozone layers, and cosmic radiation were too bizarre. How could a thin layer of ozone protect people from the deadly rays of the Sun? The instructor said that big holes were already appearing in the Earth's protective blanket.

Another thing Elliot couldn't understand was plasma. According to the instructor, plasma was invisible charged particles that moved like a gas. He said that when plasma, driven by solar winds, accelerated toward Earth at the magnetic poles, it struck molecules in the upper atmosphere and caused the northern lights. At night, the Shuttle would glow faintly, because at seventeen thousand miles per hour, the Orbiter disturbed plasma fields like a boat making waves.

Elliot had trouble understanding anything he couldn't see. He could understand water going down a pipe. He could even imagine a million little fireflies crawling down a tube. But things like electricity flowing in a wire didn't make sense to him. Nor did solar wind, electromagnetic fields, plasma, and ultraviolet radiation.

Worst of all, Elliot learned that he would be exposed to tons of radiation in space. How much radiation depended on how many solar flares were erupting on the Sun at launch time. The instructor commented rather casually, "One week of this radiation shouldn't affect you too much."

Elliot whispered to Mandy, "I'll probably come back with two noses and twelve fingers."

With launch only six weeks away, more medical tests were conducted back at the Ames Research Center. Both Elliot and Mandy dreaded this. Before landing, Elliot asked, "Mandy, don't you feel bad taking all these shots and blood tests when you probably won't get to go into space?"

Mandy shook her head. "I've still gotten to scuba dive, parachute, fly in jets, get weightless in the Vomit Comet, travel, and go through wilderness survival training. I've even gone to the bathroom in a million-dollar toilet and practiced wearing a diaper." Mandy grinned. "Plus I got to know you."

"You're the best," Elliot said.

"What, at going to the bathroom?"

"No, silly. You know what I mean."

Elliot and Mandy were glad to return "home" to the Johnson Space Center from Ames. Press conferences were held more often now. Each was a nonstop flurry of questions, flashes, and shutters. Elliot received most of the attention. One day he blurted to a rude reporter, "Hey, everybody here has trained their tails off. All you'll learn from me is stuff about me." He pointed at the other astronauts. "From them you'll learn how to save the planet. Ask them more questions!"

An awkward silence was followed by applause. Even the astronauts clapped, including Commander Beaman. He looked over at Elliot and, for the first time, he smiled.

Launch was only four weeks away now. The crew trained intensely on safety procedures and mission simulations. Each astronaut met with a dietitian. In orbit, astronauts needed about three thousand calories per day. Foods were either freeze-dried, dehydrated, thermostabilized, irradiated, or fresh. Elliot had sampled foods from the Orbiter menu and picked his favorites. "I'll take chocolate pudding, meatballs with barbecue, spaghetti, dried peaches and pears, and chocolate chip cookies," he said, feeling as if he were grocery shopping.

More and more, Elliot heard himself referred to as an astronaut. At news conferences he was introduced as payload specialist Elliot Schroeder. It still seemed unbelievable. How could an ordinary kid off a ranch near Big Timber, Montana, be a payload specialist? But the fact remained: he *was* a trained astronaut, and he *was* going into space.

The whole crew flew overnight to the Kennedy Space Center for a simulated launch in the real Orbiter on the pad. This Terminal Countdown Demonstration Test was as real as things would get before actual launch. TCDT lacked the joking and laughter of earlier training. They wore their actual orange pressure suits and helmets. Elliot knew the next time this happened, it would be the real thing.

His heart pounded as he heard the simulated countdown in his helmet. "Ten . . . nine . . . eight . . ." He imagined the thundering ignition of the Solid Rocket Boosters as he breathed in rhythm with the count. "Seven . . . six . . . five . . ." Elliot imagined the fiery reentry into Earth's atmosphere, the Shuttle's "chin" glowing like the Sun. The crazy image came to him of riding his horse, Cooper, up a ramp into the Shuttle.

The countdown kept going. "Four . . . three . . . two . . ." Elliot imagined that he couldn't get his equipment on, and the Shuttle was leaving without him. The whole world was watching him on TV and laughing at him.

The countdown hit one, and the simulation stopped. Next time it wouldn't!

After TCDT, they flew back to Texas. Each day

ticked past like a giant timer on a bomb: launch minus sixteen days, launch minus twelve days, launch minus nine days. Giddy with excitement, Elliot got diarrhea from the stress.

"You're not the only astronaut with this problem," joked the female doctor after his checkup. "Astronauts are supposed to be so tough." She lowered her voice as if telling him a secret. "You know what? They're not!"

Knowing this made Elliot feel better.

For nine months, every minute had been spent training for the mission. Now, training ended. At launch minus one week, quarantine began. Quarantine protected the astronauts from catching last-minute colds or flu bugs. The crew was split into a Red Team and a Blue Team. Each team would work opposite shifts in space. The Blue Team started going to bed earlier each day to change their sleep patterns. Now was a time to relax, review procedures, exercise, and get their heads together.

Elliot missed Mandy and her white socks. She wasn't allowed into the restricted quarantine building. They talked by phone, but that wasn't the same. Mostly, Elliot read, slept, or called his parents. Except at meals, the other astronauts kept to themselves, too. During one gathering they autographed crew photographs for one another.

At launch minus three days, the whole crew packed their bags and flew to the Kennedy Space Center. One year ago, this flight alone would have had Elliot bug-eyed and excited as a jumping bean. Now, he stared out at the distant clouds, his thoughts already in space.

**AFTER LEBOO'S DEATH,** more questions came to Vincent's mind. Did the god, Engai, make people die? Could Leboo have been saved at the infirmary? What had caused his death? Was it the lions? Was it Leboo's foolishness? Or was it the elders and the oloiboni who refused to ask for help from Sambeke? It seemed that pride was much like stubbornness. Was this also the way of the Maasai?

Answers refused to come.

When Vincent visited other engangs, much was said without speaking. Silent stares carried hurt, anger, curiosity—and also blame. Leboo's father, Kerashon, came to Vincent. The bent and feeble old man had no teeth. He gummed his words angrily. "Because of you, my son Leboo has died."

Vincent bowed with respect, offering the top of his head to be touched. He did not speak.

Kerashon shoved Vincent's head roughly. "Has guilt taken the words from your mouth?"

"No," Vincent said. "It was Leboo who called me a coward and challenged me to hunt."

"If you hunted lions the day Leboo died, then where are the ears? Where is the tail?"

Because he spoke to an elder, Vincent chose his words carefully. "I told Leboo I would hunt because he called me a coward and because I was angry. When I found the lion, it was with cubs. No longer did my anger for Leboo hold power over me. No longer were Leboo's words loud in my ears. I could not take away from the young their mother."

"Leboo was *my* young!" Kerashon shouted. "He challenged you to hunt, and you did not hunt. This proves you are a coward. You will never make a great warrior."

Vincent repeated Sambeke's words. "Is the moon a coward if you challenge it to fall from the sky and it does not fall?" He shook his head. "Hunting lions is against the laws of Kenya. Hunting lions would not have proved I was brave. It would show only that I was foolish."

Kerashon looked struck. "You call my son Leboo foolish? Give me your herding stick."

Obediently Vincent handed over his herding stick. Without being told, he bent low. He had insulted an elder. For this he would be beaten—this was the way of the Maasai. Kerashon began swinging.

The stick bounced lightly off Vincent's back as if swung by a small child. The elder's feeble strength could no longer hurt a lizard. Though the beating caused little pain, Vincent let long moans escape his mouth. It would not be right to take from the elder his angry grief.

When Kerashon finally stopped, he smiled with toothless satisfaction. "You will speak of my son with honor," he ordered.

Vincent nodded obediently. The old man carried the pain of a lost son—he meant no wrong. Pain in the heart needed to heal the same as pain in the body.

132

After that day, except during visits with Sambeke, Vincent kept his thoughts hidden. These were not happy days. Papaa grew more sick. Each day without rain brought the death of more cows. Each day filled itself with worry and fear. Across all of Maasailand people spoke of Engai's anger. The elders offered sheep that were pure white for sacrifice and prayed to Engai for forgiveness.

Vincent remembered the days of rain when Maasailand had many happy people. During those times, the changing of life brought prayers and songs. Each day carried blessings and ceremony. Always there were feasts and celebrations and laughter.

But no longer. As if covered by a great cloud, Maasailand grew dark with fear. The wind no longer carried children's laughter across the engang. Even Vincent's favorite mother, Peninah, spoke angry words, saying, "Why does Engai kill the cattle of her favorite people?"

Vincent kept to himself, herding the cows farther away each day. Only one thing brought light into his darkness. Like the stars that visited the night sky, each evening Vincent visited Sambeke at the infirmary. Sambeke showed him more new things—things that were strange to the Maasai. Together they planted a garden. Each day Vincent watched the seeds grow. This did not feel wrong.

"Someday I think you will learn to eat what you have planted," Sambeke joked.

"That is not the way of the Maasai," Vincent insisted.

"Is speaking on radios the way of the Maasai? Do the Maasai look at the stars with telescopes? Do the Maasai make electricity for light? Is this bad?"

Vincent did not know what to think anymore. Sambeke knew and did many wonderful things. But some things even Sambeke could not do. He could not make Tome allow Vincent to learn from the wood school. Nor could he keep Vincent from having to go to the ceremony Alamal Lengipaata.

In three days' time, Vincent would be made to join the other boys. They would rub red ocher in their hair like the warriors and wear warriors' ornaments. After circling the engang with chalk white paint smeared on their bodies, they would leave and spend the night alone without fences or spears to protect them. They would sing and celebrate through the night to show their courage. Alamal Lengipaata would be the last ceremony before Vincent become a warrior in the initiation of emorata, the painful initiation into manhood.

On that day, Vincent would no longer walk the path of his heart. He would follow the path of the elders and the path of the ancients. On that day, he would stand as alone as Leboo's father, who now watched his son travel the paths between the stars. Vincent would stand alone like the moon on a windy night, doing something his heart could never share.

# CHAPTER FIFTEEN

The final three days before launch, the astronauts continued to be isolated from the rest of the world. They stayed in crew quarters at the Kennedy Space Center. Each evening Commander Beaman called meetings to discuss last-minute concerns. At one meeting, the commander asked Elliot, "Well, are you ready?"

Elliot twisted at his shirt. "I guess so. I sure hope things go okay."

Commander Beaman chuckled, "That's the understatement of the century."

On the last day before launch, each astronaut had a final checkup. Elliot's parents flew in from Montana and were given blood tests and physicals. This allowed them "primary contact," which meant they could touch and hug Elliot good-bye when they visited him in quarantine. Tense smiles and dark circles under their eyes showed their lack of sleep. His mother blinked back tears. "Hurry back," she said, fussing with Elliot's collar.

"I'll go seventeen thousand miles an hour—that's faster than Cooper heading back to the barn."

His parents didn't laugh. Elliot realized they were scared, too. He hugged them. His father rested his arm around Elliot's shoulder. "We're sure proud of you, Son."

A lump blocked Elliot's throat. "Thanks, Dad."

Dalton hadn't finished. Awkwardly he spoke. "Son, this is hard for me to say." He paused. "The ranch has always been your home, but life is taking you places your mother and I never imagined."

"What are you saying?"

Dalton tilted his head back as if stretching his neck. Looking again at Elliot, he said, "Whatever you do with your life, it's okay with me. I'm behind you—even if you don't take over the ranch."

Elliot gave up trying to stop his tears as he hugged his parents.

"You'll always be our son," Angie said.

"I know that," said Elliot. Reluctantly, he watched his parents leave. He couldn't explain his feelings. He had always wanted to do something other than ranch. Now that he could, it scared him terribly.

Later, Mr. Boslow and Ms. Lopez stopped by. Not having "primary contact" authorization, they kept ten feet away as they wished Elliot a good flight. Ms. Lopez stared intently at Elliot and said, "Elliot, astronauts always think they know who they are before going up.

But then, no matter what happens, it changes their life forever. Inside, they're never the same again. Who you are, what you think you believe, all that changes. Do you understand what I'm saying?"

Elliot nodded, but he did not understand. Not yet.

After Mr. Boslow and Ms. Lopez left, Mandy stopped by. NASA had granted her permission to visit quarantine but would not allow her "primary contact," either. She approached with a small package in her hand and stopped ten feet away. "They said I can't come any closer."

"That's 'cause girls have germs," Elliot kidded.

"You wish—it's probably so you don't start hugging me. Boys are walking hormones."

They stood staring awkwardly at each other.

"I'll be here to watch you land," Mandy said, twisting at the package in her hands.

"Are you getting mushy on me?"

With a mischievous grin, she said, "No, to make sure you don't crash."

Elliot laughed. This girl with her straight brown hair, freckles, cute brown eyes, and, yes, thick white socks was his very best friend in the whole wide world.

He glanced around, and not seeing anybody, he whispered, "Mandy, hold your breath."

"Do what?"

"Hold your breath."

"Why?"

"Just do it!"

"You're crazy," she said, drawing in a breath.

Quickly Elliot ran to her and gave her a strong hug. She hugged him back.

"We're a great team," Elliot blurted.

She nodded. Still holding her breath, she handed him the package.

Quickly they separated, again glancing to see if anybody had seen them. Mandy let her breath explode. She giggled. "I'm the one who probably got germs."

"I wish you were going along," Elliot said, suddenly serious.

"Me, too." She smiled wistfully. "I better go. Good luck!"

It was hard for Elliot to watch Mandy walk away. She should be the one going up instead of him. Dazed by his feelings, Elliot opened the package. Inside, he found a brand-new pair of thick white socks. He laughed as tears came to his eyes.

Back in his room, Elliot stared out the window at the sky. Nothing seemed real anymore. All his life he had wondered what it was like to be in space. Tomorrow, he would find out.

A fitful night's sleep ended with a jarring wake-up alarm. Elliot sat up instantly—this was one day he couldn't be late. He showered and put on his blue jumpsuit. Then a knock sounded on the door. In walked a NASA assistant, looking like a space alien with a face mask and blue bodysuit. Only his eyes showed. "It's time," he said. "Are you ready?"

"I better be," Elliot said. "I stayed awake most of the night just thinking and waiting."

The masked assistant led Elliot downstairs to where all the astronauts had gathered. The crew joked very little as they sat down for an old NASA tradition: a breakfast of steak, eggs, coffee, and orange juice. Nobody ate much. After breakfast, each astronaut privately put on a diaper. Then with the help of masked assistants, they pulled on their orange pressure suits.

Commander Beaman briefed them. "Okay," he said. "Things look good for launch. Forecast calls for scattered clouds at five thousand feet; visibility eight miles; winds ten knots gusting to fifteen; temperature seventy-three degrees; dew point fifty-six degrees; humidity eighty-two percent. Any questions?"

There were none.

"Okay, let's do it!"

The press waited outside the Operations and Checkout Building with TV crews and cameras. Amid flashing cameras and shouted questions, the astronauts carried their helmets and walked single file to the van. They rode quietly to the launchpad, each crew member lost in private thoughts.

During training, the launch area had been a beehive of people and vehicles moving everywhere. Today, the pad stood empty except for the closeout crew helping load. The Shuttle *Endeavour* towered like a skyscraper with its huge External Tank and Solid Rocket Boosters. Sunlight gleamed off the Orbiter and the

SRBs. Pressurized gas drifted from vents near the top of the brown External Tank. A flock of ducks rose from a nearby marsh and flew past. Mosquitoes swarmed everywhere as usual.

Elliot tried not to think about his parents, his friends, the ranch, or Mandy. He had to stay focused. Countdown had begun many hours earlier. Yesterday the Orbiter had been powered up and the flight control systems tested. Flight-deck computers were activated and fuel cells turned on. During the night, technicians had worked installing critical equipment into the payload bay. Only two hours ago, the External Tank had been filled with liquid oxygen and liquid hydrogen.

Launch was now two hours away and counting. The astronauts of mission STS-97 exited the van and filed across to the launch tower where they entered a brightly lit elevator and rode up to the crew-access walkway. Elliot swatted at several mosquitoes trying to pierce his padded orange pressure suit. From the crew-access walkway, they entered the "white room," a loading platform beside the entry hatch. Here, assistants helped them put on helmets and prepare for ingress into the Orbiter.

Countdown had reached launch minus one hour and twenty minutes. With the Orbiter poised for launch, everything was tilted on its back. The astronauts crawled carefully through the small round side hatch and used the middeck wall as a floor. Their personal gear had already been stowed in lockers days earlier.

Using footrests and handholds, Elliot made his way to his seat. Tod Cochran and RoxeAnn Karch sat middeck. Elliot felt lucky to be sitting on the flight deck. He reclined on his back with his knees up while an assistant strapped him in. At launch minus fifty minutes, Commander Beaman confirmed with radio voice link that each astronaut was ready. When his turn came, Elliot answered, "Roger."

At launch minus forty and counting, an updated weather forecast came from an astronaut flying a T-38 jet over the cape. Winds were picking up in the stratosphere, but launch still looked good for a go.

The launch director radioed at launch minus ten that the transatlantic abort sites in Africa looked good. A knot tightened in Elliot's gut. This was no simulation. His chalky mouth was not caused by the dry oxygen flowing into his helmet.

A calm female voice announced, "We are go for launch at T minus nine minutes and counting."

Elliot stared up through the cockpit windows at the lazy white clouds drifting past. Panic gripped him. Strapped tightly into the Orbiter, he breathed faster and faster. "No!" he told himself. "Keep calm!" He forced slow breaths. Communication between Control and the flight deck sounded just like the simulation.

But it wasn't a simulation.

"*Endeavour*, this is Control. You are now on internal power, over."

"Roger, out."

"*Endeavour*, this is Control. Hydraulic check complete, over"

"Roger, out."

"*Endeavour*, this is Control. Main Engine Gimbal complete, over."

"Roger, out."

"*Endeavour*, this is Control. $O_2$ vents closed, looks good, over."

"Roger, out."

The calm female voice sounded again, "We are go for launch at T minus five minutes and counting."

Elliot licked at his dry lips and forced his breaths. The huge crew-access arm on the tower swung away from the Orbiter. Auxiliary Power Units had started up, and Main-Engine Gimbal checks were completed.

"Control, this is *Endeavour*. APU to inhibit, over."

"Roger, we copy, *Endeavour*, out."

A long silence. Elliot swallowed. He wondered if the big gaseous oxygen vent hood, the "beanie cap," had lifted off the External Tank yet.

"*Endeavour*, this is Control. $H_2$ tank pressurization okay. You are go for launch, over."

"Roger, go for launch, out." Commander Beaman spoke to the crew as casually as if they were on a Sunday drive. "If everyone's ready, close and lock your visors. Have a good trip!"

A brittle silence filled the Orbiter. Elliot checked his visor, then a terrified grin came to his lips.

"*Endeavour*, this is Control. Auto-sequence start is go. You are now on your onboard computers, over."

"Roger, out."

The woman's voice grew tense. "Nine . . . eight . . . seven . . . six . . . We have main engines start."

A deep loud rumble shook the flight deck.

Each word now made Elliot shiver as if he had touched an electric fence. "Five . . . four . . . three . . ."

**THE CEREMONY** Alamal Lengipaata was now ready to begin. Vincent could not stop the ceremony any more than he could stop the morning's sun from rising. All the boys gathered and chose a leader from their father's generation. This man, Selempo, would help them to make life's important decisions.

On the day of Alamal Lengipaata, Vincent did as all the other boys of his age group. He prepared carefully. Into his hair he smeared the muddy red ocher dye of the warrior. With ostrich feathers he prepared a head-dress. Over his legs he smeared white chalk paint. Before the paint dried, he traced patterns with his fingers.

His mothers, Peninah, Nasha, and Noonkishu, brought to him a necklace made of colored beads. His favorite girl, Nasira, also came to his small-hut. Without speaking, she placed a colored neck band at Vincent's feet. Smiling with embarrassment, she turned and rushed away. Vincent stood tall, feeling big with pride—Nasira thought him brave. This day, it was good to be Maasai.

All was ready. The boys gathered with the oloiboni and other elders. Carrying spears and walking in a long line, they circled the engang. Each boy walked straight and tall. The girls followed. Their stares and giggles made the boys walk even more tall. Vincent saw Nasira watching him. He pretended not to notice.

Two times the boys circled around the engang, leaving their spears by the small-huts. Then, led by the oloiboni, they left the engang and walked the dry countryside. All day they walked until they came to the shores of the distant Lake Kabongo. There they built a large fire.

Without the fences of the engang and without spears to protect them, the boys began their ceremony and celebration. All through the night they sang and danced. The eyes of wild animals glinted from the darkness. Some boys threw rocks and taunted the eyes. The oloiboni watched the boys closely, blessing them often.

The night did not allow rest. The boys circled the fire, holding hands and chanting. Even as the sun offered its light to a new day, the boys still sang and danced to the numbing sound of a drum. Finally the oloiboni gave his last blessing. When he finished, the boys cheered. They were ready for the initiation of emorata. Then they would be warriors.

"We shall become the greatest warriors the Maasai have ever known!" shouted one boy.

"Already we are the bravest!" shouted another.

Cheering and laughter filled the air. Vincent stood

watching the other boys. Sambeke had said that all the world was changing. He said that if the Maasai did not change they would be destroyed. He must be wrong, Vincent thought. Nothing could destroy warriors who were so strong, proud, and brave.

A tall boy named Simel gave Vincent a playful shove. "Does Vincent think of Nasira?"

Vincent smiled—he liked Simel. "And who do you think of?" Vincent asked.

"The beautiful girl, Nanta," said Simel. The tall boy let his eyes roll upward. "She is more beautiful than a bird that sings. And she thinks I am more brave than a bull elephant."

Vincent pretended surprise. "Nanta? She is more ugly than a buffalo in mud."

"And your Nasira, she is more ugly than the warthog," said Simel with a lazy grin.

"And you are as scared as a lizard without a tail."

"And you are a jackal that runs from its shadow."

Vincent and Simel laughed loudly, holding hands. Around them, other boys also joked and held hands to show friendship. This was the way of the Maasai.

The long night left Vincent tired but filled with pride. Standing taller than ever before, he joined the others for the long walk back to the engang.

When they arrived, night was near. Vincent wished to speak to someone about his night by the lake. His father was too sick to speak. His mothers were helping with the cattle and with meals. Vincent decided to visit

Sambeke. He left the engang and crossed the valley to the infirmary.

He found Sambeke talking to strange voices on his black box. Sambeke motioned for him to sit down. Vincent squirmed with excitement. Finally Sambeke hung up the handset. He did not show surprise at Vincent's dress.

"Why does the chair not let Dreamer Boy sit still? Do you have safari ants inside your toga?"

"No. I have gone with the oloiboni and the elders to the ceremony of Alamal Lengipaata. We went to the shores of Lake Kabongo. All night we sang and danced." Vincent showed off his red-ochered hair and white legs. "We have not slept for two days." He pointed proudly to his neck band. "The girl Nasira made this for me."

Sambeke listened, nodding patiently. "So, Dreamer Boy, have you decided to become a warrior?"

Vincent avoided Sambeke's eyes. He shrugged. "Papaa does not let me choose."

"But I hear excitement in your voice. What has your heart chosen?"

Still Vincent avoided Sambeke's stare. "If I become a warrior, then Papaa will not be angry at me."

"Very well," Sambeke said. "It is best I do not tell you about tomorrow night."

Vincent looked up. "What is tomorrow night?"

Sambeke pretended to be bored. "Oh, it is nothing. I do not think a Maasai warrior would be interested."

Vincent tugged on Sambeke's shirt. "What? What is happening tomorrow night?"

Sambeke smiled. "I have found out from other radio operators that tomorrow night the Space Shuttle *Endeavour* will be crossing Kenya. We will be able to hear them speak to people on the ground as they cross over. They might even speak to us. But of course this is not something a Maasai warrior would want to hear."

"A machine that travels in space?" Vincent gasped, pointing up. "We could talk to such a thing?"

Sambeke faked a yawn. "Maybe. But I'm sure a Maasai warrior has much more interesting things to do."

"I shall be here!" Vincent shouted.

Countdown for the Space Shuttle *Endeavour* continued. "Three . . . two . . . one . . . we have SRB ignition.

"And we have liftoff!"

Huge bolts exploded to release *Endeavour* from the pad. Solid Rocket Boosters suddenly belched forty-four million horsepower, echoing dull thunder as they carried a skyscraper away from the Earth. Aboard rode the world's first Junior Astronaut wearing a diaper and thick white socks.

Elliot felt as if a bull had bucked him into the air and landed him on a rough-riding freight train. After liftoff, Mission Control switched from the Kennedy Space Center to Houston. Through his helmet communication, Elliot heard the tense communications on the radio.

"*Endeavour*, the tower is clear. All engines look good. Instituting roll maneuver."

The rocket nozzles swiveled, rolling *Endeavour* over

into the proper trajectory away from the cape. Even hanging upside down, Elliot was pressed tightly into his seat by the g forces of the rockets. Barely thirty seconds into the flight, the Shuttle's main engines throttled back as *Endeavour* approached the speed of sound.

"Houston, this is *Endeavour*. Main engines at sixty-five percent, over."

"Roger, out."

The Shuttle thundered and shook as the sky turned a darker blue. In the cockpit, Commander Beaman and pilot Victor Lutz kept busy, changing abort procedures each minute as they climbed through Earth's atmosphere.

Elliot couldn't believe this was really happening. He waited anxiously for the Solid Rocket Boosters to burn out—they were supposed to last two minutes.

The shaking eased, then the announcement came, "Houston, this is *Endeavour*, we have SRB burnout; ready for SRB separation, over."

"Roger, out."

A brilliant orange flash filled the flight deck. Elliot knew the separation motors had fired, guiding the empty rocket casings safely away from the Shuttle. Soon the SRBs would deploy their parachutes and splash into the Atlantic Ocean a hundred miles downrange.

The Orbiter dipped. Suddenly, everything became smooth with only a slight purring. The sound was misleading. Outside, the Orbiter's main engines still belched out awesome power. They sucked hundreds of gallons of fuel each second from the huge External Tank.

"Houston, this is *Endeavour*. We have SRB separation."

"Roger, visual confirmation reported from Kennedy, out."

Commander Beaman sounded casual. "We are now thirty miles up, approaching three thousand miles per hour."

Elliot breathed deliberately. The speed could not be felt. Without telephone poles going by, it was like sitting in a stopped elevator. For another two minutes, he listened to the sucking sound as he breathed oxygen and gazed straight ahead. The Orbiter's main engines kept purring. Elliot waited for something to go wrong. By this time during *Challenger*'s last flight, everybody aboard was dead. It wasn't a good thing to think about, but it was true.

"*Endeavour*, this is Houston. You are negative return. Do you copy?"

"Roger, Houston. Negative return, out."

No longer could the Orbiter abort back to the launch site in an emergency. At more than four thousand miles per hour, any abort now would be transatlantic. The next command made Elliot shiver with excitement.

"Houston, this is *Endeavour*. We are single engine press to Main Engine Cut Off, over."

"Roger, *Endeavour*. You are single engine press to MECO, out."

"Yes!" Elliot grunted, hoping nobody had heard him. The transatlantic aborts were gone. Now, even if two engines failed, they could still reach orbit. Outside, the sky had become inky black. No matter what, he was going into space. He was on his way to making history!

"*Endeavour*, this is Houston. Main Engine throttle down, over."

"Roger, out."

Elliot felt the engines cutting back on their power.

"*Endeavour*, this is Houston. Go for Main Engine Cut Off, over."

"Roger, Main Engine Cut Off on schedule. Out."

As the purring of the Main Engines stopped, Elliot's arms floated up. He pulled them down and let them float back up again. "Unbelievable!" he whispered. His hands hurt from holding them in tight fists. Within seconds, he heard, "*Endeavour*, this is Houston. Go for ET separation."

"Roger, out."

A thump sounded on the hull of the Orbiter as explosives released and pushed the huge External Tank away.

"Houston, this is *Endeavour*, we have External Tank separation."

"Roger, out."

Commander Beaman spoke to the crew. "We are now seventy miles high and traveling over seventeen thousand miles per hour. We are in a direct insertion ascent profile so our momentum will take us the rest of the way up to our final orbiting altitude of two hundred fifty miles. There we will make a brief engine burn to stabilize our orbit."

For the next half hour, *Endeavour* and Mission Control spoke sporadically. Tension had disappeared from their voices. Elliot relaxed. He couldn't wait till they reached orbit and could float free.

At launch plus forty-five minutes, the Orbital Maneuvering System engines fired, easing the Orbiter into a free fall around the Earth. They traveled too fast now to come down, and too slow to go any higher. The firing jolted the Orbiter. For about fifty seconds Elliot was pressed into his seat. Then the OMS burn ended.

"Houston, this is *Endeavour*. OMS-2 cutoff. We have achieved orbit, over."

"Roger, *Endeavour*, you are in orbit, out."

Commander Beaman spoke to the crew. "Well, let's get to work."

Quickly, Elliot released himself from his harness. Like a balloon, he hung suspended. *Unbelievable!* He was floating in space! Gently he pushed away from the seat, floating. He turned to mission specialist Shannon Thorpe, suspended beside him. She smiled and glided forward. Elliot reached out and pushed on her hands. They both rolled backward. Elliot caught a handhold.

Everyone removed and stowed their helmets and pressure suits, preparing for on-orbit operations. Seats were folded and equipment unpacked. Starting now, each astronaut would struggle to follow a timeline of experiments and chores. No longer was there night and day as on Earth. Each orbit completed a ninety-minute day-to-night cycle of light and dark. Meals, sleep, and work were planned based on mission schedules. The Red Team and the Blue Team would alternate twelve-hour work periods, one sleeping while the other worked.

Shannon Thorpe guided herself down through the interdeck access hole to the middeck. Elliot peered out through the windshield at the Earth floating above them. They were floating upside down to a world that glowed and shimmered blue with white swirls of cloud. It didn't seem possible that this was the same world they had just left. Somewhere down there in the swirled colors were Mom, Dad, Mandy, and Old Crowleg. Beyond the arching blue-and-white horizon of the Earth waited the cold black of deep space. In a frightening sort of way, it was beautiful. A full moon shined big and proud like it was showing off. It had good reason, Elliot thought.

Quiet with awe, Elliot glided down the opening to middeck to start the SAREX. He unstowed a handheld receiver, a headset, an antenna, a microcassette recorder, and a power converter. With no up or down, he could eat, sleep, or work in any position he wished. Carefully Elliot set up the equipment, checking the transmitting frequency of 145.55 megahertz. He scanned five different receiving frequencies.

Elliot looked forward to this part of his mission

assignment. He could talk to anyone he wanted. Because other amateur radio operators would be listening, he reminded himself to be polite. He was now a goodwill ambassador for NASA and for the United States of America.

A check showed the Orbiter passing over east central Africa. Elliot selected an uplink frequency. After tuning and adjusting volumes for a couple of minutes, he heard a voice with an accent saying, "Space Shuttle *Endeavour*, this is 5Z4XZ in Kenya calling. 5Z4XZ in Kenya calling."

Elliot answered, "5Z4XZ, this is Space Shuttle *Endeavour*, go ahead."

An excited voice came back immediately. "Yes, Space Shuttle *Endeavour*, I am happy to talk to you! Very happy! My name is Sambeke. I am Maasai, and I am a doctor here at a small infirmary. Over."

# CHAPTER SEVENTEEN

**A**t the infirmary, Vincent squirmed when he heard the voice on the black box. Sambeke had said, "Space Shuttle *Endeavour*." Who was this? It sounded like a boy.

"I am glad to speak to you, Space Shuttle *Endeavour*," Sambeke repeated. "I welcome you to our skies. Over."

"It's good to be over Kenya," said the voice on the box. "Our orbit is two hundred and fifty miles up. We're very near to you, over."

"Yes, we are near but very far apart," said Sambeke. "Many people in the world are this way, I think, over."

Vincent nudged Sambeke's knee. "Can I speak to the boy?" he pleaded.

"It is not a boy," Sambeke whispered. "It only sounds like a boy. They do not take children into space."

"It *is* a boy," Vincent insisted. "Can I speak to him?"

Sambeke nodded. "Space Shuttle *Endeavour*," he said. "I have a friend, Vincent, who asks to say hello."

Excitedly Vincent picked up the handpiece.

Holding down the lever, he spoke loudly. "Hello! I am Vincent Ole Tome. What is your name?"

"5Z4XZ, my name is Elliot Schroeder."

"Are you just a boy?" Vincent blurted.

Sambeke grimaced at the question.

"I'm fourteen years old," Elliot replied. "I'm the first Junior Astronaut in space. How old are you?"

"I have also lived fourteen years." Vincent spoke to Sambeke. "Is he really up in the sky?"

Sambeke pointed up. "He is so far up that he floats like a hawk on the wind."

Vincent shook his head. "How can that be?"

"He's in a spacecraft."

Vincent kept shaking his head even as Sambeke motioned for him to speak again. "Elliot," Vincent blurted. "If you are in a spacecraft, then you are a space-boy. I do not think that is possible."

Elliot chuckled. "It's hard to believe, but that's where I am. Where exactly are you? Over."

"I am with Sambeke, near our engang. Over."

"What I mean is, where in Kenya are you?"

Vincent spoke more confidently. "Spaceboy Elliot, I am only one day's walk from Tanzania."

"In the Narok district," Sambeke whispered.

"In the Narok district," Vincent added. "Over."

"Roger. What nationality are you?"

Vincent looked to Sambeke and whispered, "What does he mean, nationality?"

"He wants to know what culture you are."

"What do you mean culture?" Vincent pleaded, feeling as if he had no brain.

"Tell him you are Maasai," Sambeke instructed.

"Spaceboy Elliot, I am Maasai. What are you? Over."

"I'm American, but my parents are part German and part Danish, over."

"How can that be? Are their feet German and their ears Danish? You must look funny. I am all Maasai, nothing else."

The boy on the spacecraft, Elliot Schroeder, replied bluntly, "What I mean is that some of my ancestors were German and some were Danish, that's all. Over."

Vincent spoke louder. "If I marry someone who is not Maasai, my papaa will say I am not his son. He does not like the Kalenjin, the Kikuyu, or the Kisii. If I marry someone else, I forget the ways of the Maasai. So tell me, what are the ways of the German and the Danish? Over."

"Uh, I don't really know because we live on a ranch up in Montana. Some of the older people get together. They fix special foods and stuff like that. Over."

"So, Spaceboy Elliot, if you have forgotten the ways of your elders and the ways of the ancients, then tell me, what do you do now?"

"Vincent, we do plenty. We go to town for pizza some Fridays. At school sometimes we have dances. Evenings and weekends I help my dad and mom with chores like taking care of the cattle or helping put up the hay we grow. I take flying lessons. I do lots of stuff. So, what does a Maasai person do? Over."

Vincent spoke more strongly. "Maasai people do many things. We are not like a cow who only grazes. We believe in Engai, the god who made all that is. The Maasai herd many cattle and do not dig in the ground because the ground is sacred—it gives us grass for our cattle. Papaa says that a person who digs in the ground is weak and a coward—they are Potato People and are our enemy. We never dig in the ground. Over." Vincent did not admit that he had helped Sambeke plant a garden.

"Roger, 5Z4XZ, we dig in the ground to plant crops. This makes more grow. We dig to build houses and lots of things. How do you bury your dead? Over."

"We leave our dead to be eaten by the hyenas and the lions. What do you do with your dead? Over."

"We bury our dead in boxes under the ground—that's the civilized way. Over."

"You are very selfish to not give back to the ground what it has given you. If you dig in the ground, then you are a Potato Person and should not have cattle, over."

"Why shouldn't we have cattle? Over."

"Papaa says that Engai gave all the cattle in the world to the Maasai. So, if you have cattle, I think you have stolen them from the Maasai. Over."

"Vincent, you're crazy," Elliot said. "First off, we don't believe in this Engai god you're talking about. We have our own god called God. He is the only god. We didn't steal your cattle. Besides, you don't own every cow in the world. What do you think we did, steal your cows, then swim them across the ocean? Another thing—digging in the ground doesn't mean somebody is a weak coward. Over."

Vincent laughed as he spoke. "If you do not know the ways of your elders and the ancients, how do you know your thoughts hold truth? I think if I ever find your cattle, I will steal them back. They are not yours!"

Elliot spoke bluntly. "That's cattle rustling. I don't care if you're Maasai or who you are, if you ever try to steal our cattle Dad will turn you in to the sheriff. You'll end up in jail! You'll never—"

The radio fuzzed and took away the spaceboy's voice. With the handset in his tight fist, Vincent turned to Sambeke. "Where did he go?"

Sambeke spoke quietly. "It is only possible to speak to the Space Shuttle for a short time. Because the Shuttle orbits the Earth every ninety minutes, and because it takes the world twenty-four hours to go around, the Shuttle will not pass over us again until tomorrow at this time. Perhaps you can speak to the young astronaut, Elliot Schroeder, again then."

Vincent hardened his voice. "I do not know if I want to speak to Spaceboy Elliot again. The spaceboy's words prove he is not a friend of the Maasai or somebody to trust. He does not believe in Engai. He is a Potato Person. He has stolen our cattle. And he is not Maasai. I think he is my enemy."

Sambeke smiled the way the elders smile when they know more than they can explain. "Dreamer Boy, is it hard to speak to one's enemy?"

Vincent nodded.

Sambeke pointed to his ear. "You will find it is even harder to listen to one's enemy."

"Why is that?"

"Because it is always possible that your enemy's words might hold truth."

"But, Sambeke, what if I know—"

Sambeke held up his hand. "Dreamer Boy, it is time for you to leave. Sleep with your questions. Maybe answers will come to you without my help."

Vincent stood obediently and picked up his walking stick and spear. "Good night, Sambeke."

Sambeke smiled and led him out the door into the gathering darkness. "Good night, Dreamer Boy. Come back again tomorrow if you dare listen to your enemy," he said.

Vincent waved but said nothing. Alone, he walked back across the dark valley. Two times he stumbled as his eyes searched the sky above. Somewhere up there was a Potato Boy who stole cattle and did not believe in Engai. How could this person not be his enemy?

When Vincent arrived at the engang, his favorite mother, Peninah, met him.

"I need to see Papaa," Vincent said. Tonight he needed his father to tell him that the ways of the Maasai were the only right way.

Peninah shook her head slowly. "The oloiboni and the paangishu's medicine have not helped your father. He still breathes, but tonight he has fallen into a sleep from which he does not awake."

# CHAPTER EIGHTEEN

**E**ndeavour's trajectory had carried them out over the Indian Ocean. It would be another twenty minutes until contact could be made with somebody in Australia. Elliot kicked the bulkhead. Why had he lost his temper talking to the Maasai boy, Vincent Ole Tome? He hoped that not too many other radio operators had heard. The Maasai boy should mind his own business.

RoxeAnn Karch motioned to Elliot. "Let's get your medical work started."

Reluctantly, Elliot held himself steady while RoxeAnn took vital signs. After taking his blood pressure and pulse, she drew blood and gave him some kind of shot. Finishing, she said, "Every four hours, Tod or I will run these tests. Be sure to let us know if you feel ill or strange in any way."

"I already feel strange," Elliot said.

"How so?" RoxeAnn asked, her voice concerned.

Elliot grinned. "I feel like I'm weightless and floating around the world at seventeen thousand miles per hour."

RoxeAnn smiled and put away the test equipment, then floated upward to the flight deck. Blue Team was still asleep. Red Team moved about, working to keep up with their timeline sequence of duties. Elliot kept working with the SAREX, talking next to a man in India and a woman in Portugal.

Later in the work shift, Elliot took a quick break and floated up to the flight deck to look outside. The Shuttle had reached the dark side of the Earth. Far to the north an eerie glow pulsed like a giant halo over the polar region.

"I think that's the northern lights," Elliot exclaimed, pointing out the flight-deck window.

RoxeAnn turned to look from where she floated near the remote-arm control panel in the aft crew station. She nodded. "That's the aurora borealis. Pretty."

"It's radiation, isn't it?"

"Yup. Those are particles from a solar wind hitting molecules in the upper atmosphere. Imagine the folklore and legend those lights have caused."

Elliot pointed back through the rear windows of the aft crew station into the Shuttle bay where the huge bay doors stood open. "And what's that?" he asked. A strange orange glow blanketed the rear edges of the Shuttle and drifted off into space.

162

RoxeAnn motioned out the window. "Look, Victor. Elliot has spotted some Shuttle glow."

Shuttle pilot Victor Lutz turned to look. RoxeAnn floated to face Elliot. "At more than seventeen thousand miles an hour, the Shuttle disturbs the plasma in space. This bathes the Shuttle in electrical charges and causes chemical reactions."

Elliot didn't understand what she was saying but he sure wished that Mandy and Mom and Dad could see all this. Reluctantly, he returned to the SAREX. One by one, he spoke with people around the world. This time, he made contact with Argentina, Spain, New Zealand, and Israel. Each contact stammered with excitement to be talking to the Space Shuttle. Elliot kept a list of call signs. Back on Earth, he would mail each a confirmation card with a picture of the Shuttle *Endeavour*.

The first work cycle went smoothly. After talking on the SAREX, Elliot held his first television question-and-answer interview with a network of schools. It was hard to believe that a million students were watching and listening to every word he said. Before ending, he waved at the camera and said, "Hi, Mandy, wherever you are!"

After the interview, he prepared the evening meal of Salisbury steak and vegetables for Red Team. He called it the evening meal only because it was the third meal of the work period, and that is what it would have been had this day started and ended in Florida. But already the mission had experienced a half dozen day-to-night cycles.

During the first sleep cycle, Elliot didn't sleep much. He kept thinking back to his first conversation with the Maasai boy in Africa. How could Vincent Ole Tome know anything about someone in Montana? Burying dead people didn't make someone a Potato Boy. Nobody had stolen any cattle. And Elliot sure didn't believe in the god Engai that Vincent Ole Tome talked about.

All of Elliot's life he had gone to the Lutheran church in town. In Sunday school, church, and at home, he had been taught to pray to God. Sure other people believed there were different gods, but Elliot had always been taught that there was only one god— his god. It wasn't Engai. It was a good thing Vincent lived on the other side of the world.

At the end of Red Team's first sleep cycle, payload specialist Tod Cochran woke Elliot for more tests. Elliot found his hands floating out away from his zipped-up sleeping hammock. He felt like Frankenstein's monster. "Do you have to take blood tests each time?" he grumped, unzipping himself from his sleeping hammock.

Tod Cochran nodded. "We'll call you the Pin Cushion."

"Great!" said Elliot, bracing his body.

When they finished, Elliot brushed his teeth and wiped his body down with a wet washcloth. Then he floated away from the middeck sleeping quarters to the flight deck. Victor Lutz worked alone. Commander

Beaman and Shannon Thorpe had gone to sleep mid-deck.

For five minutes Elliot stared out the windows at the gigantic blue-and-white Earth drifting magnificently past. Somehow this wasn't quite what he had expected. It was much neater. Elliot couldn't help but wonder how the barn cats from the ranch would act floating around up here. The thought made him smile.

The Shuttle gave no sense of motion. Only the sounds of blowers and equipment marked the passage through space. Once in a while something clinked against metal. Twice, pilot Lutz fired small clusters of rockets in the Reaction Control System. The RCS rockets caused the Shuttle to roll, yaw, or pitch. Always the Earth drifted past like a giant turning globe.

Returning to work, Elliot set up the SAREX equipment again and talked to six people across the United States, Canada, France, and Saudi Arabia. After glancing at his watch, Elliot looked at the ground-track map to see where he was approaching next. He paused and fingered his pen. *Endeavour* was coming up on Kenya, Africa, again. It had been twenty-four hours since the first communication with the Maasai boy Vincent Ole Tome. Something made Elliot want to call Vincent again. If for no other reason, to tell him he was a jerk.

Hesitantly, Elliot looked up Vincent's call sign. He set the frequency and pressed the microphone lever. "5Z4XZ, this is Space Shuttle *Endeavour*, over."

Immediately other ham operators tried contacting

the Shuttle, but Elliot ignored them and waited for a reply from 5Z4XZ. Again he tried, "5Z4XZ, this is Space Shuttle *Endeavour*, do you read? Over."

The radio crackled loudly, "Yes, Space Shuttle *Endeavour*, this is 5Z4XZ. Is this Spaceboy Elliot? Over."

Elliot hated being called Spaceboy Elliot. It made him sound like a cartoon character. Deliberately he said, "5Z4XZ, this is Elliot Schroeder aboard the Shuttle *Endeavour*. Is this Maasaiboy Vincent Ole Tome? Over."

"Yes, Spaceboy Elliot, this is Vincent. Have you decided to give back my cattle? Over."

Elliot stared with disbelief at the SAREX radio. The bonehead! Elliot wished he could flush their toilet over the top of Vincent, but the particles would only vaporize on reentry. Because other ham operators were listening, Elliot tried to keep his talk professional. "I read you loud and clear. I haven't taken anything that's yours. I've never said you have the wrong god, or called you names like Potato Boy. So why do you say that to me? Over."

"Spaceboy Elliot, Papaa tells me the white man has tried to take our land for many years. For many years the white man has come and told the Maasai they have the wrong god. I have seen this happen with my own eyes. So now I know you are also a liar. Over."

Elliot sat speechless for a moment. When he spoke, he spoke forcefully. "Maybe somebody else has done that to you, but I haven't. Do you understand?"

"Papaa has taught me the ways of the Maasai. He has also told me the ways of the white man. The white man always thinks he is right."

Elliot pinched his handset hard and blurted, "Not all white people act that way. Besides, you told me that your god, Engai, was the only god. You think you're the one right about that. Over."

"Spaceboy Elliot, there is only one god. Engai made the sky, the ground, the air. Engai made all people. Engai forgives. If I am real, Engai is real. Can you hear my voice, Spaceboy? If you can, it proves Engai is real. Unless you think I am a spirit. Over."

The radio fuzzed out Elliot's reply as the Orbiter *Endeavour* glided out across the Indian Ocean toward another cold and inky black night cycle.

# CHAPTER NINETEEN

In Africa, the Maasai say that even a small tree gives some shade for rest, but Vincent's life gave him no shade. Each talk with Spaceboy Elliot made Vincent more angry. Papaa grew worse, and still more cattle died. To help Papaa, the oloiboni killed a sheep for sacrifice to Engai. The paangishu brought healing herbs each day. Still Papaa did not move except for his hard breaths. Sweat came to his face like the heavy dew on a morning leaf.

Vincent knew he disobeyed his father and brought him no respect when he did not hunt for lions and elephants. But the hungry cattle needed more herders now.

Still each day carried Vincent closer to the day of emorata when he would become a man. This he did not mind. But emorata would also make him a full warrior. This would carry Vincent farther from the wood school. Farther from learning the magic of Sambeke.

He begged of his mothers that he not be forced to

become a warrior. He asked also if Sambeke could visit Papaa. His mothers Nasha and Noonkishu refused. They said it would not be Papaa's wish and it would not honor the ways of the Maasai. Vincent's favorite mother, Peninah, answered only with her sad and silent eyes.

If life were not already cruel, now anger also kept Vincent awake at night. He could not forget his visits with Sambeke and his talks with the spaceboy. Why would the spaceboy think the ways of the Maasai were wrong? Vincent planned well his next words to Spaceboy Elliot.

The next night, he corralled the cattle quickly so he could visit Sambeke's. Before leaving, he grabbed a drink of goat's milk and a gristly chunk of goat's meat from Peninah's small-hut. Soon, he knocked on the door of the infirmary.

Sambeke greeted Vincent. "Ah, Dreamer Boy."

"Has Spaceboy Elliot spoken on the black box yet?" asked Vincent, breathing fast.

Sambeke motioned for Vincent to sit down. "Perhaps he will not call. Why should he? So he can hear you argue again?"

"But, Sambeke, he tells me the ways of the Maasai are wrong. He does not believe Engai lives."

"And what have you told him?"

Vincent shrugged.

"You have told Elliot Schroeder his god does not live. You have called him Potato Boy and accused him of stealing your cattle."

"But what I say is true."

"Ah," Sambeke said loudly. "So now you are the only one who knows what is true."

"But it is true!" Vincent insisted.

"When a zebra runs from a lion, which one does wrong?"

Vincent puzzled at the riddle. "They both do what they know. One is a lion and one is a zebra."

"And you are a Maasai, and Spaceboy Elliot is a white man. He asked you how he could have stolen cattle and crossed the ocean. Has your mind answered that question?"

"I do not care how."

Sambeke worked to adjust the switches and knobs on the black box. "So truth does not ask you to think, huh?"

Vincent grew angry with Sambeke. "Papaa is right. You think the ways of the Maasai are wrong."

Sambeke shook his head. "I do not think the ways of the Maasai are wrong or right. What is right and wrong? Is it what you feel? Is it what you have been told? Is it what brings power? Is it what brings happiness or hurt? Can the white man's ways be right for him but wrong for you? Can that be?" Sambeke handed Vincent the handset.

Vincent ignored Sambeke's questions and squeezed the button on the handset. "Space Shuttle *Endeavour*," he said. "This is 5Z4XZ. Over."

For nearly five minutes, Vincent kept calling. Then

he heard the faint crackled reply, "Yes, 5Z4XZ, this is Space Shuttle *Endeavour*. Over."

"Hello, Spaceboy Elliot. I did not know if you would talk to me again. Over."

"Yeah, well, I wasn't so sure you would talk to me, either. Maybe we'll do better this time. Over."

Vincent swallowed before he spoke—today he must not let his words hold anger. "Yes, we will do better, Spaceboy Elliot," he said cautiously. "So, tell me. In the United States of America where you live, are you so rich you have no problems? Over."

Spaceboy Elliot laughed. "We have plenty of problems. Most years we don't make enough money to make ends meet on the ranch. Over."

"So, Spaceboy Elliot, when you are grown, what will you do? Over."

"My dad wants me to ranch all my life like everybody else has in our family for the last hundred years. But each year more ranches go broke. Things are changing. I want to become a pilot. Over."

Vincent nodded. "Yes. My papaa wants me to live the way of the Maasai. He wants me to become a warrior like all the other boys. But the ways of the Maasai are also changing. I want to go to the wood school—they study strange things that I want to understand. Maybe I could become a doctor like Sambeke. But it costs three cows to go to the wood school for one year. This makes Papaa very angry. He says when the rains come again, we will not have three cows in all the herd. Over."

"Roger, Vincent. I think our dads would get along great. How about your mom? What is she like? Over."

"Spaceboy Elliot, I have three mothers. Which one do you ask about?"

"Three mothers! Are you kidding? How can you have three mothers?"

"Nasha is my birth mother. But Papaa has married three wives. My mother Peninah is my favorite. She is very kind. She thinks much and knows much more than she speaks. How many mothers do you have? Over."

"I only have one mother. In the United States it's wrong to have three wives. Over."

"Spaceboy Elliot. Why is it wrong to have three wives? I do not understand the white man. Over."

"Well, just because. Besides, why would you have three wives?"

Vincent did not have to think to answer. "Because we have much work at the engang where I live. Also, there are many more women than men because of wars and because of wild animals that kill the herders. If the Maasai people are to stay strong, then all women must be mothers and have children. Over."

"But don't your moms get jealous if they love your dad and he's with someone else? Over."

Vincent looked at Sambeke for help with this foolish question. Sambeke shrugged and whispered, "The white man, too, sometimes has many wives. They call it divorce."

Vincent spoke strongly. "Spaceboy Elliot, I do not understand how you think. Love is not selfish! The

Maasai believe that to love, one must share. My friend, Sambeke, says that the white man also has many wives. Do you not have something called divorce where a man can have many wives? Over."

"Sure we have divorce, but that's not the same. You divorce one person before you marry another. Over."

"I do not understand, Spaceboy Elliot. What is the difference if you have three wives all at once or at different times? If I hold three balls together or one at a time, I have still held three balls."

There was a pause, then Elliot's voice came back strongly, "That's not the same. It's just not the same. Besides, we have almost as many men as women. Our men don't get killed like yours."

"Ah, I think white men must live very lazy lives with little danger if they do not get killed."

"We don't live easy. It's just that we don't go out hunting a lion with a spear. We'd use a high-powered rifle with a scope."

"So, you think if we had this high-powered rifle you speak of, then I would not have three mothers? You think funny."

"That's not what I meant. I'm not thinking funny, you're just turning things around. Over."

Vincent had one question his mind had planned. He breathed deeply and asked, "Spaceboy Elliot, if you do not think funny, then why does the white man wear pants? The Maasai wear sheets they can use for many things. Over."

"I don't know. Maybe it covers you up better. I'd hate to be running around in a dress like a girl."

"Spaceboy Elliot, why would you look like a girl? I have seen pictures. Many of your girls wear pants. What does the white man hide and cover? I think I know why you wear pants. Over."

"We wear pants because it's proper. Why do you think we wear pants?"

Vincent giggled as he spoke, trying not to look at Sambeke. "I think the white man wears pants so that he can trap his gas."

"You're nuts!" Elliot exclaimed. "I'm not exactly sure why we wear pants, but it sure isn't to—"

The transmission fuzzed and crackled and cut out. Space Shuttle *Endeavour* was once again out of range. Vincent hung up the handset and spoke. "Sambeke, the white man thinks with only half a brain. He does not know why he does what he does. That is why he always fights with other people."

Sambeke watched Vincent patiently. "The Maasai also have fought others for many years, Dreamer Boy."

"Against people with only half a brain that cannot think."

"Tell me, Dreamer Boy. Why does the Maasai travel many miles to find wood for his fire when wood lies everywhere on the ground?"

Vincent answered proudly, "Because under the wood the insects make their home. If we use the wood on the ground, it will take away the insects' home."

"Ah, so it is respect for life?"

"Yes," Vincent answered. "That is the way of the Maasai."

"If the Maasai respect life so much, then why do the warriors try to kill the sleeping lion and the elephant? Why does a man beat a wife who has prepared the evening meal late? And why cannot a woman speak on the elders' council? Have women no tongues? Have they no wisdom? These are also the ways of the Maasai."

Vincent had no answer. He did not like it when the boys killed Olarani. He hated when elders beat their wives. Many women, like Peninah, had much wisdom. In truth, there were many things Vincent did not like in Maasailand. His words stumbled from his lips. "I cannot answer because I do not understand all the ways of the Maasai."

"Ah, Dreamer Boy, what will I do with you? You search always for new thoughts, but when you find one, you hide from it like the dik-dik. No eye is so blind as the one that will not be opened. Today you asked many good questions of Spaceboy Elliot. Why did you finish by telling him he traps his gas?"

Vincent lowered his head with shame. "I must go before all the sky is dark," he said, using words to escape Sambeke's questions. He left without looking back.

When Vincent arrived at the engang, Peninah waited for him. Her eyes were wet with tears. Hesitantly she asked, "Will Sambeke come to see your father?"

Vincent showed surprise. "Yes! Sambeke will help anyone who asks. But will you let him?"

"Tonight death waits very close beside your father's bed. If Sambeke visits, the elders will be angry. They will blame Sambeke for Tome's death. They will say that—"

"But what if Papaa can be helped?" Vincent interrupted.

Peninah smiled sadly. "Then the oloiboni and the paangishu will say their powers and medicine have worked. They will still say Sambeke has tried to cause trouble. Whatever happens it will not help Sambeke. But it might help your father. This I believe."

"Then I will go and ask," Vincent said, turning to leave.

Peninah grabbed his arm. "You must not go tonight when you cannot see the lions."

Vincent pulled away. "Is it better if I go in the morning after Papaa is dead?" He left quickly and let his legs run fast like the white man. Tonight he did not want to let time pass. Tonight he ran to help Papaa.

# CHAPTER TWENTY

A board the orbiting Shuttle, Elliot jogged on a treadmill twice each day. Elastic straps held him on the moving track. RoxeAnn taped small wired patches all over his body. "Keep your pulse above one hundred forty beats per minute," she instructed. After talking to the Maasai boy, Elliot ran so hard his pulse reached two hundred beats per minute.

"What are you doing?" asked RoxeAnn, as she floated past. "Trying to run your way to China?"

"We're probably already there!" Elliot snapped, running even harder. Suddenly he felt an oozing glob of something creep across his back. He stopped and called to RoxeAnn, "Hey, something's crawling on my back."

RoxeAnn secured an instrument and floated over for a look. She laughed. "You're running so hard, sweat collected in a big blob. Surface tension is letting it creep around your back. Here." She pulled out a towel and padded up the sweat. "Something has you worked up."

Elliot mopped his brow without answering. Vincent angered him. For a while it had seemed they had something in common with their dads wanting them to follow family tradition and all. But then Vincent started talking about having several mothers, stealing cattle, Potato Boys, and wearing pants to trap gas. If everybody in the world was this weird, no wonder countries didn't get along. Elliot decided not to talk to Vincent again.

After running, Elliot felt sick. The barf bags NASA supplied were like those on the airlines, except the top had cloth around it so you could wipe off your face. Elliot had just opened the bag when he threw up. The vomit wasn't terrible-smelling like on the ground, and it didn't look like the food had digested much.

RoxeAnn came over to help Elliot. "Don't worry about it," she said. "It's just space sickness." She gave Elliot two pills. "A couple of these will help."

Medical tests continued every four hours. Elliot started sleeping better. On the fifth day all the astronauts gathered for a television interview beamed back to Earth. They even spoke to the president. After the interview, Houston kept communication open with the crew. "*Endeavour*, we have someone who wants to speak with payload specialist Elliot Schroeder," they said.

Surprised, Elliot pulled on a thin wire headset that left his hands free. "Go ahead, Houston," he said.

A crackly girl's voice came over the radio. "Elliot, how are your white socks doing? Over."

"Mandy!" Elliot almost screamed. "What are you doing? Over."

"Just checking to see if you're still wearing your socks. Over."

Elliot laughed. "I'm still wearing them. If I don't change them soon, I'll be able to use them as heat shields during reentry. Over."

"That would be air pollution." Mandy's voice sounded excited. "Elliot, I sure do miss you. They said I could just say hi, so I have to go. Hurry back, okay. Over."

"Good-bye, Mandy. I miss you, too." Reluctantly, Elliot took off the thin headset.

Commander Beaman motioned to Elliot. "I want a word with you on the flight deck."

Swallowing, Elliot nodded and floated up the ladder. He waited nervously alongside the pilot's seat. Soon Commander Beaman joined him. Floating upright to Elliot, he asked, "So, how is it going?"

"Good. Am I doing everything right?"

Commander Beaman nodded. "Houston thinks so."

Elliot glanced out at the giant Earth. They were just leaving a night cycle. For several seconds before the sun rose, the dark Earth looked wrapped in a thin red blanket. Then the sun blinked into view with a blinding flash, and the atmosphere became fuzzy white.

Elliot squinted. He knew there was a reason for this conversation. He asked, "And how do *you* think I'm doing?"

"I think you've done outstandingly." Commander

Beaman pointed out the side window at Europe. "It's hard to believe that's the soil Leonardo da Vinci stood on when he looked up at the sky and said, 'We *can* fly!'"

"People probably thought he was nuts," Elliot said, pausing. "So, why did you want to talk to me?"

Commander Beaman cleared his throat. "Not much up here is a secret. NASA has uplinked conversations you've had with a young Maasai boy. Do you know who I mean?"

"You mean Vincent Ole Tome?"

Commander Beaman nodded.

"How did they hear us?"

"It seems that a ham radio operator in Nairobi has recorded every conversation you had with this boy. He's released the tapes to the press."

"You mean people are hearing *every* word we said?"

"The press worldwide has been airing those talks in full. It's become a big thing."

"I'm not talking to him anymore."

Commander Beaman rubbed his chin. "NASA has an interest in the repeated contacts you've had with this African boy. I'd suggest you do talk with him again."

"Why? He keeps trying to pick a fight."

Commander Beaman chuckled. "From the tapes I've heard, I'm not sure he's the only one doing that."

Elliot avoided the commander's gaze.

Commander Beaman continued. "There is talk at NASA about arranging for the two of you to meet after landing."

Elliot spoke sharply. "Meet Vincent? But why?"

"Your talks have caught people's imaginations."

"What if I don't want to meet him?"

Commander Beaman frowned. "Meeting him may not be your choice. Are you afraid?"

"I'm not afraid of him."

"Then why are you getting hot under the collar?"

"He tells me everything I do is wrong. Last time he said I was dumb for wearing pants."

Commander Beaman allowed a slight smile. "So, *why* do you wear pants?"

"Because up here, a dress would float up around my face!"

"And how about on the ground?"

"Boys are supposed to wear pants," Elliot said, his face growing warmer.

"Says who?"

"Says every person I've ever met. I don't see you wearing a dress or a sheet."

"That's because it's not a custom in the United States. But I agree with Vincent. Wearing pants has to be one of the dumbest customs we have, especially in hot weather. Imagine how useful it would be if we wore sheets. You'd already have a blanket, a sunshade, something to carry things with, and you could wrap it tightly or loosely, depending on how hot the weather is." Commander Beaman moved past Elliot and settled into his flight seat.

"You're starting to sound like Vincent," said Elliot. "Whose side are you on, anyway?"

Commander Beaman flipped a couple of switches. "So that's what it is, huh? An issue of right and wrong? An issue of sides?"

"He called me Potato Boy because my dad plants crops and because white people bury their dead. He said my god can't exist because his does."

"And what do you think?"

"It's his god that doesn't exist!"

"I'll be curious how you two settle that one." Commander Beaman looked at his watch. "I've got work to do. Good luck."

Elliot returned to middeck. Shannon Thorpe met him with a video camera. "Let's do your interview with the schools," she said. "I thought a tour of the Orbiter might be fun. I'll follow you and do the filming."

"Okay," said Elliot. Moments later, with earthbound students asking questions, he gave a tour of the Shuttle.

"What does it feel like being up there?" one student asked.

"Being weightless is like going over the top of a roller coaster," Elliot answered, not knowing how to really describe the awesome feeling.

After the interview, Elliot did cabin chores. He cleaned the galley, then wiped down the bathroom with antibacterial solution. He stowed garbage in a special locker beneath the middeck floor. Chores weren't exactly fun, but it sure beat mucking stalls back on the ranch.

Elliot kept an eye on his watch. After chores, he

floated aft to set up the SAREX equipment. He didn't feel like talking to Vincent Ole Tome, but now he had to.

"5Z4XZ, this is Space Shuttle *Endeavour*, do you read me? Over." Elliot hoped nobody would answer.

No such luck. After only three calls, the faint but clear reply came back, "Space Shuttle *Endeavour*, this is 5Z4XZ. Is this Spaceboy Elliot?"

Elliot stuck out his tongue at the handset—the world wouldn't hear that. "Yes, 5Z4XZ, this is Elliot. So what's new? Over."

"What's new?" Vincent's voice sounded puzzled.

"I mean what's happened since yesterday? Over."

There was a pause. "Spaceboy Elliot, my papaa is very sick. Last night Sambeke visited him and gave him medicine. The oloiboni did not like Sambeke visiting Papaa, but I think it will help. Over."

"I'm sorry to hear about your father. Who's this oloiboni guy? Is he like a witch doctor? Over."

"No, he is a great healer and a wise man. But he has not been able to help Papaa. Over."

"Then why does he care if somebody else tries to help? Over."

There was a long pause. "The Maasai think that if the oloiboni cannot help Papaa, then Engai wants Papaa dead. Over."

"That's kind of how it is in the United States. If the doctors can't heal somebody, they say it is God's will if the person dies. Over."

"Spaceboy Elliot, if Papaa is sick and is not helped, I

do not think his death is the will of Engai. Over."

"No, Vincent, I agree with you. I really hope your father gets well. Over."

"Yes, that is what I wish also." Vincent paused. "Spaceboy Elliot, after talking to Sambeke, I think I should not have said all the things I have said to you. Sambeke says that if a zebra and a dik-dik laugh at each other, they will never eat side by side. Maybe he is right. Over."

Awkwardly Elliot answered, "I think if we lived near each other, we would be friends and get along. Over."

"Yes, Spaceboy Elliot, I think you are right—we would be friends. I think we would hold hands often. Over."

"Uh, I'm not sure we would hold hands, but we would be friends. Over."

"Why would we not hold hands if we were friends? Over."

"Well, Vincent, in the United States, sometimes girls hold hands, but boys aren't supposed to. Over."

"I do not understand the ways of the white man. Why do you not hold hands? Over."

Elliot rolled the handset nervously in his hands, not knowing what to say.

"Spaceboy Elliot, can you hear me?" Vincent asked. "Why do you not hold hands if you are friends? Over."

Elliot answered strongly. "Vincent, it's something we just don't do. Okay? Over."

"It is something you should do. I think if we ever meet, I will hold your hand. I think it would be—"

Vincent's reply was cut short by the fuzzing sound that showed *Endeavour* was once again out of range. For a long moment after losing Vincent's signal, Elliot turned and stared at the other astronauts working. He ignored the constant calls from ham operators trying to contact the Shuttle.

He realized he had his fists doubled. Why did talking to the African herder bother him so much? Even today, when most of their talk had been friendly, he found himself mad. There was no way in the world he would walk around holding hands with Vincent Ole Tome.

fter taking Sambeke's medicine, Vincent's father, Tome, slept harder and his breaths came easier. When he awoke, he could raise his arms again. His skin no longer shined brightly.

As Vincent sat watching his father, new thoughts came to his head without being asked. The oloiboni and the paangishu made medicine from the trees and the plants. Many times this medicine worked. Even Sambeke had used this medicine. But Sambeke also used the white man's medicine. Vincent had seen that work many times, too. Why did the oloiboni not want help from the white man's ways? Did not the ways of all people hold some good?

Vincent wished his mind would not ask questions without giving answers. He knew that many of the white man's ways were wrong—this he knew for sure. White men came from Nairobi, their bodies fat and teeth bad from the food they ate. Sometimes they cheated the

Maasai. The white men did not give back to the earth what they took. They buried their dead in boxes. The white men did not believe in Engai. Yes, all these things were wrong.

But Vincent had also seen the magic of the white man. Sambeke's black box could speak to a spaceboy. Sambeke had a microscope that let the eye see things that could not be seen. Vincent had listened to his own heart beating. Sambeke's loud generator machine made light without fire. All these things were made by people who were not Maasai. Did this make them bad? Vincent cradled his head in his hands. If the white man's medicine saved Papaa, was it bad? Did the oloiboni want Papaa to die?

Peninah entered the small-hut and nodded to Vincent. Tome looked up at her. Voice cracking, he said, "The heat has left my body. Make a gift for the oloiboni."

Peninah bit at her lip, then said, "The oloiboni did not help you."

Tome blinked, letting the words soak into his ears. "I am awake," he said gruffly. "Again I can think. Soon I will stand. Why do you say the oloiboni has not helped me?"

"When the oloiboni could not help you, I asked Vincent to bring Sambeke."

"Sambeke? He has been here?"

Peninah nodded. "It is Sambeke who has made you well."

Tome's cheeks twitched. "I did not ask for Sambeke to come here."

"You did not ask to be sick," Peninah answered.

Tome drew a deep breath, then shut his eyes once more. His breathing relaxed, and his chin rested against his shoulder. "I am tired," he said.

Quietly Vincent and Peninah left the small-hut. Outside, Vincent looked at his mother with a worried look.

Peninah smiled. "Do not worry. Your father's anger soaks into the ground like the rain. Let him sleep."

Vincent saw that his shadow fell long like the shadow of a tree. He looked across the valley. It was time to go and speak to Spaceboy Elliot.

Peninah saw his look. "Vincent, what do you do when you go each night to see Sambeke?"

Vincent did not have time to explain. "Come," he said. "I will show you."

Peninah paused, but nodded. "I will go and see what takes you from your family and away from the engang."

As they walked out across the dusty valley, Vincent spoke fast, telling about the spaceboy.

Doubt showed in Peninah's eyes. She shook her head. "This is a trick. A young boy does not fly above us from the other side of the world."

"You will see," Vincent exclaimed.

Sambeke saw them coming and stood waiting in the door of the infirmary. He spoke in the Maasai language of Maa so that Peninah could understand. "Ah,

Dreamer Boy, you have brought your mother. Has she come to speak to the Space Shuttle *Endeavour*?"

Vincent spoke excitedly, pointing. "She does not think there is really a Spaceboy Elliot up in the sky. Make her believe, Sambeke."

"One does not *make* someone believe. Vincent, close your eyes tightly," Sambeke ordered.

Vincent obeyed.

"Now you cannot see me. So, am I not here?"

"No, you are here," Vincent said, opening his eyes. "Let Peninah hear Spaceboy Elliot speak. That will show her."

"That will prove nothing. Spaceboy Elliot could be under the floor hiding. He could be a trick." Sambeke pointed at Vincent's forehead. "Your head must decide what is real." He motioned. "Come inside."

Sambeke walked over to the black box. As he turned it on, he spoke. "Nobody can make anybody believe anything. People close their minds to truth the way your eyes were closed to the light."

Peninah spoke quietly. "I wish to thank you for giving medicine to Tome. Today he speaks and sits up."

Vincent spoke. "Papaa thinks the oloiboni has healed him and not you."

Sambeke turned dials on the black box. "Truth does not hide itself from people," he said. "It is only people who hide from truth."

Vincent looked at the disk on the wall that Sambeke called a clock. "Can we speak to Spaceboy Elliot now?"

Sambeke shrugged. "Maybe he has not crawled under my floor yet."

Vincent ignored Sambeke and picked up the handset. "Is the black box ready?" he asked.

Sambeke nodded. "This is a ham radio, not a black box."

Vincent spoke loudly in English. "Space Shuttle *Endeavour*, this is 5Z4XZ. Over."

With Sambeke translating each word for her, Peninah watched, her eyes opened wide like a gazelle.

"Space Shuttle *Endeavour*, this is 5Z4XZ. Can you hear me? Over," Vincent repeated.

Several more times Vincent tried before the sharp crackle of Elliot's voice came back, "Yes, 5Z4XZ, this is Space Shuttle *Endeavour*. I hear you loud and clear. So, what are we going to argue about today? Over."

"Spaceboy Elliot, maybe we will not argue. Today my mother Peninah is here, and—"

"Ask him where he is," Peninah told Vincent.

"My mother wants to know where you are, Spaceboy. Over."

"Peninah, this is Space Shuttle *Endeavour*. We are in orbit two hundred and fifty miles above Kenya."

Sambeke translated the words. Peninah looked to Sambeke. "Two hundred and fifty miles? How far is that?"

"From here to Nairobi," Sambeke whispered.

Peninah shook her head. "That is ten days' walk. How can he be ten days' walk up in the sky?"

"He is, Mamaa! He is!" Vincent spoke into the handset. "Spaceboy Elliot, my mother does not believe you are ten days' walk up in the sky. Over."

Vincent heard Elliot laugh. "Roger, Vincent. You couldn't get here by walking. Tell your mom I'm traveling over seventeen thousand miles per hour."

With Sambeke translating, Peninah looked startled. "Seventeen thousand miles per hour? What does the spaceboy say?"

Sambeke laughed. "He is traveling so fast, he could be to Nairobi in less than one minute."

"What is a minute?" Peninah asked.

"How long it takes you to walk around the infirmary," Sambeke said.

"This is a trick," Peninah said.

"Spaceboy Elliot, my mother does not believe you can travel ten days' walk in less than one minute."

"Well, I can't exactly step down and prove it. By the way, have you gotten any rain? My dad says it's real dry back in Montana. Over."

Vincent shook his head. "No, Spaceboy Elliot. Engai is angry. It has been very long since Engai shook her garments over Maasailand to bring the rains. Over."

"You called Engai a her. Is your god a woman?"

Vincent thought a moment. "Yes, Spaceboy Elliot. Engai is a woman, or a man. It does not matter. What is your god?"

"Our god is a man."

"How do you know?"

"All the pictures I've seen show him as a man. It

would be weird having a god that was a woman. Over."

Sambeke tapped Vincent on the shoulder. "Ask Elliot who took the pictures of his god?"

"Spaceboy Elliot, who took the pictures of your god? Over."

"Nobody really took pictures. They just drew pictures of what they thought he looked like. Over."

"Spaceboy Elliot. We have not seen Engai, so we do not draw pictures of her. Over."

"Yeah, but you can imagine, can't you? Over."

"I do not know how you look. If I draw a picture of you, it will not be right. Why should I draw a picture that is not right? Over."

"Vincent, how do we end up talking about such weird stuff? I don't care what God looks like."

"Then why do you draw pictures, Spaceboy Elliot? How do you know your god is a man? Over."

Elliot's voice sounded louder. "If somebody asked you what you thought Engai looked like, would you have her ugly or good-looking? Would she have short hair or long hair? Would her skin be black or white? What color would her hair be? Don't you ever think of stuff like that?"

Vincent spoke strongly. "Spaceboy Elliot, Engai would not be ugly. She would be black because she is Maasai. She would have no hair because hair makes a woman ugly. Only the Maasai warrior has long hair. Does your god have long hair? Over."

There was a long pause. "Yes, our pictures show God with long hair. Over."

"Then I think your god is a very ugly woman. Or he is a Maasai warrior. Nobody else has long hair. Over."

"God is *not* a woman! He's *not* a warrior! And he's *not* Maasai! Do you understand? Over."

"Ah, Spaceboy Elliot. You say you have not seen your god. So how do you know he does not have black skin? How do you know he is not a woman? And why would he have long hair if he is not a warrior? Over."

Elliot sounded angry. "I've prayed to God, and he's not Maasai. I do know that. Over."

"Spaceboy Elliot. You have talked to me also. Do you know how I look? Sambeke said today that truth does not hide from man—it is man who hides from truth. Why do you hide, Spaceboy Elliot? Over."

"Oh, for Pete's sake, Vincent, I'm not hiding from you or Sambeke or from truth or nothing. You're weird to have a woman god with no hair. You're the one with an ugly god. You're the one who is hiding from truth. This is *Endeavour* signing off. Over and *out!*"

Sambeke took the handset from Vincent. Gently he spoke. "Space Shuttle *Endeavour*, this is 5Z4XZ. Do you hear me? Over."

There was no answer.

Again Sambeke spoke, "Space Shuttle *Endeavour*, this is 5Z4XZ; you and Vincent must not end your talk this way. Can you hear me? Over."

A crackling static filled the room. Slowly Sambeke

hung up the handset and shut off the black box. He looked at Vincent with a hurt look.

Vincent looked down.

"You are afraid of Spaceboy Elliot," Sambeke said.

"I am not afraid of the white boy," Vincent snapped.

Sambeke spoke deliberately. "Many people have heard the words that you and Elliot spoke this night. You have shown everyone why the world has always known war. Old people are like the dead tree that no longer changes except to rot. Change will not come from the elders. After listening to you this night, I am not sure it can come from the young, either."

"But, Sambeke, Elliot said that—"

Sambeke held up his hand. "I am tired, and the sky grows dark—it is time for you to leave." Sambeke nodded to Peninah and spoke in Maa. "I am glad for your visit. I am also glad that Tome feels better. Wish him well from me." He nodded to Vincent. "Good night, Vincent."

"Why do you not call me Dreamer Boy?" Vincent asked.

"Because dreams cannot come true without change. Good night."

# CHAPTER TWENTY-TWO

**G**lad to be out over the Indian Ocean, Elliot busied himself cleaning and offering packaged drinks to the crew. He was too angry to speak to other ham radio operators. When he finished, he glided forward on the middeck and up the access ladder to the flight deck.

Commander Beaman sat behind the flight console. He spoke to Houston like a robot. Spotting Elliot, he motioned to the pilot's seat. "Go ahead and sit in Victor's seat if you want—just don't touch anything."

Elliot lowered himself into place.

Commander Beaman turned. "So did you speak to your Maasai friend again?"

"He's not my friend," Elliot said.

"People everywhere, from bars in Dublin to ghettos in America, are tuning in each day to hear your talk with the Maasai boy. It's become a regular soap opera."

"What's the big deal?"

Commander Beaman shrugged. "You've got everybody arguing about the same things you two argue about. The same things that countries have gone to war over for thousands of years."

Elliot tried to remember all he had said that day. What he remembered did not make him proud. "I guess I kind of shoot my mouth off a bit, huh?" he said.

Commander Beaman kept flipping switches on the console. He allowed a rare chuckle. "You two do fail to communicate. Something about that boy scares you."

"I'm not scared of Vincent," Elliot said. "He just makes everything I do seem dumb. It's him that's dumb."

"Could it be that neither of you are dumb? Maybe you need to understand how this Vincent thinks."

"What do you mean?"

"In college I studied Maasai culture. Western civilization thinks differently than they do. Our culture wants only to know *how*. *How* to go faster. *How* to earn more. *How* to make faster computers. It's the reason we're in space—to learn *how*."

"So, how does a Maasai person think?"

"They ask *why*. *Why* should we go faster? *Why* should we own more? *Why* should we even have computers? Even though I'm a Shuttle commander, I think *why* is always the better question. Even a baby's first question is *why*, not *how*. Maybe this will help you understand Vincent better."

"But he's the one who called me Potato Boy and said our cattle were his."

"So it's all *his* fault?"

Elliot frowned. "You think it's *my* fault?"

"Look out there." Commander Beaman pointed at the thin haze blanketing the blue planet Earth like fuzz on a tennis ball. "Our atmosphere is all that protects us from deadly outer space. Just below the surface, Earth is hot molten lava that would cook us in a second. Five miles up or five miles down, we could not exist."

"What does that have to do with Vincent and things' being my fault?" Elliot asked.

Commander Beaman pointed to a large island off the coast of Africa. "That's Madagascar."

Elliot could see the brownish island below them. Extending out from each inlet were dark reddish plumes of dirty water, reaching for miles into the ocean like smoke. "It looks like something bleeding to death," he said.

"It's a country bleeding to death. Their topsoil is washing away because of all the trees they cut down."

"The fools," Elliot muttered.

"Don't blame them—they're just surviving. You would do the same thing."

"So, whose fault is it?"

"We're the ones buying all their exotic timbers."

"Buying wood isn't wrong," Elliot argued.

Commander Beaman shook his head. "An American person wastes a hundred times more of the world's resources each day than a person from Madagascar. They can't change much or they would die. So it *is* our fault. We could change, but we don't. We're too spoiled and comfortable."

"What does this have to do with my talk to Vincent?"

"It's easy to think other people's ways are foolish or odd, but life has evolved over millions of years. The Maasai ways have allowed them to survive in Africa. Their lives actually make more sense than ours. Our ways have let us become addicted to TV. We're the ones with the most crime and drug use. We're the ones with the most obesity and mental illness.

"Everything the Maasai do is based on survival and has good reason. They have bald heads because it's so hot and dusty in Maasailand. They wear togas for the same reason. As a culture they would not have survived without multiple wives. We have a multimillion-dollar dental industry and still have horrible teeth. Their toothbrushes are little sticks they cut from trees. With nothing but these sticks and very few sweets, their teeth are healthy."

"It sounds like you're on their side," Elliot said.

"Our side! Their side!" Commander Beaman said abruptly. He pointed up through the windshield at the lazy blue sphere floating past against the inky black of outer space. "Look at that planet!" he ordered. "Do you see any boundaries or borderlines? Well, do you?"

"No, I guess not."

"Boundaries exist only in our minds. That world

is everyone's home. Hurricanes, typhoons, drought, sunlight, pollution, air, everything exists without boundaries. We're all fellow travelers on a great spaceship floating toward a common future no one can imagine."

Elliot had never heard Commander Beaman speak like this. He kind of understood what the commander meant. The longer they orbited, the less he felt like a Montana ranch boy. He hardly felt like an American citizen anymore. He felt like just a person from the Earth. A very tiny person. "So, do you think we should live like Vincent?" Elliot asked. "Is that what you're saying?"

"Earth is on a *countdown*. If we don't wake up and take care of this planet, life as we know it will end." Commander Beaman paused. "I memorized something once for a tenth-grade speech project. It was written by a great Indian chief named Chief Seattle. He said, 'There is no quiet place in the white man's cities. No place to hear the unfurling of leaves in the spring, or the rustle of insects' wings. What is there to life if a man cannot hear the lonely cry of the whippoorwill or the argument of the frogs around the pool at night?'"

Commander Beaman stared out at the stark blue sphere of Earth as he continued. "Chief Seattle said, 'If man spits upon the ground, he spits on himself. The Earth does not belong to man—man belongs to the Earth. All things are connected like the blood which unites one family. Whatever befalls the Earth befalls the sons of the Earth. Man did not weave the web of life; he is merely a strand. Whatever he does to the web, he does to himself.'"

Commander Beaman let his words hang in the air. He and Elliot sat looking out at the Earth in silence.

Thoughts tumbled through Elliot's mind. He thought about Vincent. He thought also about his own god and about the god Engai. He thought about the muddy waters pouring from the island of Madagascar and about the wafer-thin layer of air surrounding the shining blue Earth. Chief Seattle's words made sense. "Man did not weave the web of life; he is merely a strand. Whatever he does to the web, he does to himself."

Suddenly Mission Control broke the quiet. "*Endeavour*, this is Houston—we have a problem! We show atypical cooling levels in flight-deck consoles CRT-2, F7, O6, and in AV BAY 1, 2, and 3. Confirm these readings."

Immediately Commander Beaman snapped into action. He scanned the panels, flicking toggle switches and jotting down readings. "Roger, Houston," he announced. "This is *Endeavour*. Readings concur. We will begin immediate shutdown of unnecessary electronics."

"What's wrong?" asked Elliot.

"Return to middeck!" snapped Commander Beaman. A stiff tension in his voice replaced the soft and haunting words of Chief Seattle. He barked into the intercom, "Victor, report to the flight deck!"

Elliot pulled free of the pilot's seat. Almost immediately, pilot Lutz floated from middeck and lowered himself into place. Elliot glided down the access ladder.

In minutes Commander Beaman came on the crew intercom. "Attention, this is Commander Beaman. As you know, this is the first mission using the new fluid cooling system for the Orbiter's computers. We think a micrometeoroid has struck a coolant loop on the bay door. We have lost avionics cooling in AV BAY 1, 2, and 3 and cooling to our console computers. In addition, an electrical surge has left us with only half power on the emergency cooling fans.

"This Orbiter is one huge floating computer. If we have no computers, we have no control. All experiments requiring the use of onboard computers will be terminated immediately. Unnecessary electronics should be shut down. Ambient cabin temperatures will be lowered. All computer inspection panels should be removed to aid circulation."

Elliot floated near the bunks, staying out of the way. He glanced toward his feet at the white, but dirty, good-luck socks Mandy gave him. Now he would need them.

He glanced at his watch. SAREX equipment didn't use a computer. Maybe he could talk to somebody. Barely had he started toward the equipment when the announcement came from the flight deck. "This is Commander Beaman. Temperatures continue to climb in our onboard computers. Houston has declared an in-flight emergency."

For two hours NASA's emergency teams and the crew of Space Shuttle *Endeavour* worked feverishly with Mission

Control. Their guess had been right. A micrometeoroid had impacted the left bay door. Coolant seeped out from the Orbiter like drifting snow.

Finally Commander Beaman announced grimly to the crew, "Houston is aborting the mission. Landing sights in the U.S. are under bad weather. Trajectory or bad weather prohibits our landing in Morocco, Spain, or Germany. Decision has been made to land *Endeavour* on the west coast of Africa at Dakar, Senegal. The soonest our trajectory will allow a landing is fourteen hours from now. Let's hope our computers keep running that long.

"If not, God help us!"

# CHAPTER TWENTY-THREE

Vincent spoke little with his mother after leaving the infirmary. He kicked at the dirt as he walked toward the engang. Above, the moon tried to hide behind scattered clouds that drifted with the night wind. Again and again, Sambeke's words repeated in Vincent's head, "Dreams cannot come true without change."

"I do not fear Spaceboy Elliot, and I do not fear change," Vincent muttered to himself.

Before going to her small-hut, Peninah turned to Vincent, her face heavy with worry. "Vincent, do not tell your father about the spaceboy. Old minds can drown with new thoughts."

Vincent nodded. Spaceboy Elliot no longer mattered. Only a fool would go up into space. Only a fool would eat foods from the ground. Only a fool would wear pants to trap his gas. Only a fool would think Engai was not real. Vincent went to his bed, as the restless sounds of the cattle pushed into the small-hut.

When morning touched the sky, it found Vincent still tired. Today would be long—already the cows bawled with hunger. Vincent pulled open the gate. Once free of the corral, he drove the cattle hard in the early light. If they feared his walking stick, they would think less of the hollow hunger that pulled at their bellies.

Soon the hot sun rose, bringing choking dust. Vincent glanced at the flat umbrella trees inviting him with their shade. He turned his head away. This was not a time for foolish thoughts.

Rushing the cows made Vincent think of the white man. Elders said the white man always rushed because he did not know how to let time pass. Today, Vincent could not *make* time pass. The hot sun seemed like a turtle crossing the sky. The day threatened to last forever. Even the clouds that came each day with their empty promise of rain refused to come.

Dust covered all of Vincent's body when finally the tired sun crawled toward the mountains and stretched the shadows long on the ground. Vincent's legs felt like branches on a dead tree. His tired mind struggled to carry thoughts. Tonight he would not go to see Sambeke. Tonight he would not waste his time speaking with Spaceboy Elliot. This he had decided.

He whistled hard to start the herd moving back toward the corral and the engang. Faintly he heard a dull thumping noise—probably a machine Sambeke called a helicopter, taking rich white men from Nairobi to see the animals of the Maasai Mara. Vincent searched the sky. Far away the helicopter appeared like a bee in the air. It flew toward the herd. The sound grew louder, and Vincent stopped to watch. As the flying machine came in low and fast, the cows turned in circles, their eyes wild. Vincent shouted and drove the herd forward—he did not need to lose cows to make this day any longer.

The machine flew past but circled. Vincent waved his walking stick angrily, to motion the machine away. The flying machine disobeyed and landed.

The cattle lunged against each other, frantically pushing and stumbling. Vincent picked up rocks and threw them at the helicopter. The rocks fell short. He tried again to drive the herd away.

"Wait, Vincent! Wait!" shouted a voice above the shrill whine of the flying machine.

Vincent turned and stared in disbelief. It was Sambeke running toward him from the helicopter. Behind Sambeke ran Tiyo, one of Vincent's younger brothers.

"Wait, Vincent!" Sambeke shouted.

The cows bawled, desperate to be away from the flying machine, away from their hunger, and away from their fear. Fear alone could kill a weak cow.

Sambeke ran up, breathing hard. "Your brother Tiyo will drive the herd to the engang. You must come with me."

Tiyo did not stop to talk to Vincent. Walking stick in hand, he ran directly to the herd and started driving them.

"What is happening? What is wrong?" Vincent asked.

"We will talk as we fly. Come quickly." Sambeke pulled Vincent's arm and ran toward the shiny helicopter.

Vincent stumbled forward, trying to glance back at Tiyo. His brother had the herd moving, running from side to side to keep the cows together.

"Something has happened," shouted Sambeke, ducking under the spinning blades.

Vincent backed away from the big machine, but Sambeke pulled him firmly. "It will not hurt you," he shouted. He helped Vincent crawl into the helicopter and motioned for him to sit in a chair with soft padding. Sambeke clipped a strap around Vincent's waist.

"What is wrong?" Vincent screamed, scared to tears by this strange thing that was happening.

The helicopter roared louder as Sambeke crawled into the chair beside Vincent. In the front, a black man sat at a small wall of switches and lights and glass circles—things Vincent had never seen before. The man wore white man's clothes and he had a funny round calabash strapped over his head.

Vincent stiffened as the machine shook and the ground moved away. He gripped the sides of the padded seat with all of his strength. Below, Tiyo drove the herd. Vincent blinked hard to see through the dust. Soon the cows looked like insects.

Sambeke leaned close, shouting, "The Space Shuttle *Endeavour* has had an emergency. They cannot land in the United States because of bad weather. If they do not land soon, they will crash. They have decided to land in Dakar, Senegal, on the west coast of Africa."

"But why do you come for me?" Vincent hollered, staring down at the moving ground.

"The United States National Aeronautics and Space Administration has decided they want you to meet Spaceboy Elliot when he lands in Senegal."

"Me? Why?" Vincent could not believe what he heard. "Papaa will not let me go."

Sambeke patted Vincent's knee. "I have talked with your father today. Peninah has made him understand that I have helped him live. She has also made him see that what happens to you, it is like the rain. It is something that Engai wishes."

Sambeke pointed to himself. "Tome has said I must go with you to Senegal. We will land first at the engang. Your father wishes to speak with you. Then we will fly to Nairobi where a United States Air Force jet will meet us. It will soon be dark. We must be in Dakar, Senegal, by the time the sun comes up tomorrow."

"I still do not understand. Why me?" Vincent yelled.

"That I cannot explain. Are you afraid?"

Vincent shook his head but he lied.

Sambeke pointed. "There is the engang."

Vincent looked down and shouted, "It cannot be. I moved the herd all day. We have not come far enough."

Sambeke smiled. "We are not herding cows now."

Vincent sat stunned. The helicopter changed sounds as it landed. Dust boiled up. Word of Vincent's flight had bounced from lip to lip like a ball. Many Maasai from other engangs stood watching, their mouths open.

Sambeke helped take away the strap from around Vincent's waist. The man controlling the flying machine opened the door. "Hurry," he said. "The air force jet is waiting in Nairobi."

Vincent ducked under the swinging blades as he left the flying machine. He pretended not to notice the stares. Peninah met him with a fresh toga and cow-skin sandals in her hands. "Here, you must be clean," she said.

"Mamaa, why does Papaa let me go with Sambeke in the flying machine?"

Peninah smiled. "In Maasailand, the man is the head of the engang, but the woman is the heart. Today Tome has listened to the heart. Go and change, then speak with Tome. He wishes to see you before you go."

"Is he angry with me?" Vincent asked.

Peninah shook her head. "He is frightened."

"Of what is he afraid?"

"Death has tried to visit his small-hut and has made him scared." Peninah hesitated. "When death comes close, one learns to love all that is. Tome is afraid of your leaving. Death has made him afraid you will not return."

"I will return. I go only to meet someone I do not like."

Peninah smiled. "You have much to learn about enemies. Enemies do not know each other. I think Elliot is someone you know very well."

"Spaceboy Elliot has said that—"

Peninah placed her fingers against his mouth to stop his words. "Your enemy is the one who stares up at you from calm water. Change now, then speak to your father. When you finish, I will give you meat and cow's blood. If I cannot satisfy your mind, I will satisfy your belly." She pushed him lightly. "Move fast. This day does not wait for you."

Vincent changed garments, then went to his father's small-hut. Tome sat waiting out front.

"Papaa," Vincent said fearfully, lowering his head to be touched. "You asked to see me."

Tome touched Vincent's head softly with his bony hand. His voice sounded stronger. "Tell me, my son, what is very short but can reach any fruit?"

"A bird," Vincent said, trying not to show his eagerness to leave.

"What has legs but cannot walk?"

"A stool."

"What wakes all people?" Tome asked.

"The morning."

"What is it that never rests, day or night?"

"The water from the spring."

Tome raised his head and looked up at Vincent. "And what is the warrior like when he stands on one leg?"

Vincent wanted to answer "A toadstool," but that would anger Papaa. Obediently he said, "The candelabra tree."

Tome did not blink. "My son, you are Maasai, of this I am sure. You know the ways of the Maasai well, so I do not understand why you leave."

"Papaa, many of the white man's ways are bad and make me glad to be Maasai. But some are magic. That is what I go to see."

Tome reached out his gnarled fingers and touched the ground. "The white man wants only what the hand can touch." He closed his eyes and bowed his head. "The Maasai want what the heart can touch." Tome opened his eyes. "Tell me—if my son leaves, will he come back?"

"Papaa, you have said the eye that travels becomes wise. Sambeke will bring me back."

"Sambeke will bring back your body. But will he bring back your mind? Will he bring back your heart? When you let go of a monkey, does it return?"

"Papaa, a monkey does not belong in a cage."

"And where does my son belong?" Tome asked firmly. "Is this engang a cage?"

Vincent lowered his gaze and spoke quietly. "You ask

a riddle I cannot answer, Papaa. I am too young."

Tome's voice softened. "A goat's skin helped your mothers carry you as a child. That same skin must also help you to carry your mothers when they are old. Believe my words—the elder who sits on the ground sees more than the child in a tree." He spread his arms wide. "This engang, these people, this is your place. This is the water that gives you life. You cannot drink the rain which still falls."

Vincent took a breath and spoke. "Papaa, you have told me the will of Engai is like sleep. You do not find it, it finds you."

Tome allowed a slight smile. "Even a blind sheep sometimes finds water."

Vincent looked toward the waiting flying machine. "Papaa, if you tell me not to go, I will obey—I am your son. But without your words, I must go. All that is happening would not be so if Engai did not wish it so."

Tome sighed. "You cannot feel the pain of a thorn in my foot, but I feel your pain as you go. I will not stop you. But if you go, let it be the will of Engai. Promise me only this. Promise me you will not let the white man's ways destroy you like the fire that tempts the insect to fly near."

Vincent nodded solemnly. "I promise you, Papaa, I will not let the white man's ways destroy me."

As Vincent turned to leave, Tome asked, "If you have little milk and many to share it with, what do you do?"

Vincent laughed. "Sprinkle it with cow dung."

Tome smiled. "Yes, that will make people drink very little." He waved Vincent away. "When you return, do not bring smoke and say that it is dust. I will wait to hear you speak truth of your travels."

"I will speak the truth, Papaa. I promise." Vincent rose to his feet and left the engang.

Peninah waited with Sambeke and the man who made the helicopter fly. Sambeke wore his Maasai toga and not the white man's clothes—this Vincent had never seen before.

"We must leave," Sambeke said.

Peninah handed Vincent a small calabash of cow's blood and a large chunk of raw goat meat. "I say good-bye here because I am afraid of the flying machine," she said. Speaking more quietly, she said, "Tome has told me something he has not told you. He said he knows you have courage, perhaps more than any other son."

"Then why am I so scared?" said Vincent.

Peninah smiled. "Those who walk alone know fear as surely as a foot grows wet when it walks through the dew of a morning grass. No one has courage as great as the one who knows great fear."

"Thank you, Mamaa. I will take your words with me as I have taken the meat and the blood." Vincent turned and walked toward the flying machine that would take him to Nairobi, a place he had never seen. There, something called a jet would fly him to Senegal, a place he had never heard of before today. Then he would meet Spaceboy Elliot.

Vincent tried to swallow his fear, but he could not. And he could not swallow his questions. Was the spaceboy his enemy? Or was Spaceboy Elliot someone who would hold his hand?

# CHAPTER TWENTY-FOUR

After declaring an emergency, the Shuttle swarmed with activity like a beehive smacked with a stick. Priority experiments received frantic last-minute attention. Tons of gear needed to be stowed. Like free-floating robots, everyone spoke in abrupt serious tones. Rushed movements had to be deliberate. Twice Elliot tumbled across the middeck when he missed a handhold.

Several hours after the emergency started, Commander Beaman announced, "Elliot, report to the flight deck."

Elliot puzzled as he floated forward. Why would he be called to the flight deck now? What had he done wrong?

Victor Lutz and Commander Beaman sat in the cockpit, exchanging mind-numbing amounts of technical information. Elliot floated behind them and hung suspended.

The Shuttle had traveled into a night cycle, and strong muted flashes from a lightning storm on the Earth's surface jumped from cloud to cloud. Elliot stared at the mushrooming flashes.

Commander Beaman took off his earphones and turned. "Elliot, someone's meeting you in Senegal."

"My mom and dad?" Elliot asked.

Commander Beaman shook his head.

"Not Mandy!" Elliot exclaimed.

"No, the Maasai boy, Vincent Ole Tome."

"What? I don't understand. Why would—"

Commander Beaman held up his hand. "Your talks with the Maasai boy have drawn huge public attention. NASA has decided it would be good publicity to fly Vincent Ole Tome from Kenya to the landing sight in Senegal." Commander Beaman kept working, flicking switches and checking gauges. "Personally, I think this is something that should wait until after the emergency."

A new kind of fear gripped Elliot. He had faced angry bulls in a pasture. He had ridden miles through freezing blizzards. Now, he had even gone into space. But nothing seemed as bad as having to meet this crazy Maasai boy. Not even an emergency landing.

As Commander Beaman pulled his earphones back on, he said, "Just keep in mind, millions of people will be watching."

Elliot nodded and floated down the access ladder. Middeck, payload specialist Tod Cochran had removed forward lockers to expose the main computers.

RoxeAnn Karch had a small fan rigged to blow air across the computer boxes.

Elliot remembered an instructor describing the Shuttle as a hundred smaller machines made up of bolts, turbines, seals, washers, hinges, cables, and computer chips, all working together and depending on each other. Still it seemed hard to believe that a few small black boxes could force the Shuttle down.

Elliot gave apple energy bars to everyone at their work stations. He wondered, did Mom and Dad know *Endeavour* was in trouble? Did Mandy know? She'd be glad she hadn't made it into space. Although, knowing her, she'd still want to be here. Elliot remembered asking her if she'd be scared going into space. She had said, "No, I'd go up even if I knew I wasn't coming back."

There was no time for sleep now—Red Team and Blue Team remained awake with the emergency. The temperature was lowered further on the middeck to help cool the computers. *Endeavour* needed computers during every second of flight. The computers were being fed data needed for landing in Senegal. Reentry angles, speeds, coordinates, everything would need to be changed if they were going to make it down in one piece. The crew wore jackets as they prepared *Endeavour* for reentry. Even the smallest items needed to be secured.

Elliot made dozens of trips to the equipment bay, stowing gear. Time passed quickly. Before it seemed possible, Commander Beaman announced, "Crew members, prepare for landing."

RoxeAnn floated up to Elliot. "Would you mind unstowing the pressure suits?" she asked.

Elliot nodded and guided himself forward. Tod Cochran worked reattaching the lockers. One by one, Elliot removed the pressure suits and handed them out. Before pulling on his own, he floated the last two suits up to the flight deck. Landing seats had been locked back into place.

When Elliot finished suiting up, he strapped himself tightly into his seat. He sat motionless, thinking. Did white good-luck socks work if they stank? He sure hoped so.

As Elliot waited, he kept thinking about Vincent. Why didn't he want to talk to the Maasai boy? Was it because they were so different? Did everyone want them to get into a fight like two boxers? Would that prove who was right?

One thing really bugged Elliot. Vincent had said the white man's ways were wrong. Well, white people lived a million different ways. Besides, what would a Maasai boy know about people who lived half a world away?

As Shannon Thorpe strapped herself into the seat next to Elliot, Commander Beaman announced, "We are at landing minus one hour and forty-two minutes and counting. Preparing for deorbit burn."

Elliot stared straight ahead and listened to Victor Lutz and Commander Beaman go through checklists.

"Helium pressure vapor isolation switches closed."

"Tank isolation switches open."

"Cross-feed switches closed."

Both Victor Lutz and Commander Beaman were on automatic mode now, turning dials, snapping switches, checking meter readings, and talking like computers. Commander Beaman flipped a row of switches. "Check left Reaction Control System."

"Open tank isolation," Victor Lutz said.

"Reaction Control System cross-feed switches off."

Commander Beaman spoke louder. "Houston, this is *Endeavour*. Auxiliary Power Unit prestart complete, over."

"Roger, *Endeavour*, this is Houston. APU prestart complete. Out."

The checklist continued until Commander Beaman announced, "We are at landing minus one hour and seventeen minutes. We are waiting for a go or no-go decision from Houston for our deorbit burn."

The radio crackled, "*Endeavour*, this is Houston. You are go for deorbit burn. Over."

"Roger, this is *Endeavour*, we are go for deorbit burn. Out."

Victor Lutz's face stiffened with tension. He maneuvered *Endeavour* around so the Shuttle orbited tailfirst. Finishing, he announced, "Houston, this is *Endeavour*. Maneuver to burn attitude complete. Over."

"Roger, *Endeavour*. Houston, out."

Commander Beaman flipped several more switches

and turned a valve handle. After checking indicators to his left, he said, "Houston, this is *Endeavour*, we have single APU start. Over."

"Roger, *Endeavour*, single APU start. Houston, out."

"Houston, this is *Endeavour*. Orbital Maneuvering System engines are armed, over."

"Roger, OMS armed. Houston, out."

Elliot bit at his dry lips. The deorbit burn coming up would only slow them down about two hundred miles per hour. At more than seventeen thousand miles per hour, that didn't seem like much. But slowing just a little allowed gravity to capture the Space Shuttle and start reentry.

Commander Beaman pushed keys on the computer keyboard, beginning countdown. "Houston, this is *Endeavour*. Countdown to OMS burn ignition: five . . . four . . . three . . . two . . . one . . . ignition. Over."

"Roger, ignition. Houston, out."

There was a jolt, then for several minutes Elliot felt a gentle vibration and pressure on his body from the OMS burn. Just as quickly, the burn ended, then all was still again.

"Houston, this is *Endeavour*. OMS burn is complete. Over."

"Roger, *Endeavour*. Burn complete. Houston, out."

Commander Beaman announced to the crew, "We are at landing minus fifty-four minutes. Our OMS burn was successful. Now, one way or another, we're coming down!"

ear, curiosity, and weariness all struggled to control Vincent's mind as the helicopter shook its way across the Kenyan countryside. Light from the setting sun made the colors deep and rich.

Sambeke pointed. "That is the Great Rift Valley."

Vincent nodded but was not listening. A short time ago he had been far from the engang, fighting with a hungry and restless herd. Now he flew above the ground toward Nairobi in a flying machine. He dared not think about meeting Spaceboy Elliot tomorrow. Not yet. His mind could not hold all that happened today. Papaa once said that each day must worry about itself.

"There is Nairobi," Sambeke said pointing. "The name means *cold place.*"

Vincent stared. Could it be? Sambeke had spoken of

Nairobi, saying it was a thousand times bigger than any engang, with small-huts taller than hills. But from the sky, the small-huts looked no bigger than those the children made of dirt.

The helicopter banked sharply in the gathering darkness.

"Do you feel okay?" Sambeke asked.

Vincent nodded and swallowed, afraid to open his mouth to answer with words.

They dipped toward a flat strip of land so straight it looked like Engai had reached down and scraped it with her own hand. Soon they landed with a sharp jolt.

When he stepped from the flying machine, Vincent reached down and touched the ground. It was smooth and hard as stone.

Sambeke smiled. "It's called asphalt."

Vincent saw people gathered. Most were Africans, but they wore white man's clothes. Vincent puzzled. Were they Maasai, Kalenjin, Kikuyu, Kisii, Luo, or what? How was he to know? He stared up at a huge square small-hut nearby. Bright lights lit up the air. Here, they did not need the sun.

"That is the main terminal building," Sambeke said.

Vincent and Sambeke ducked low and ran out from under the big blades that still turned above them. Several men met them. They wore green clothes and carried guns. "Follow us!" they shouted.

Sambeke motioned Vincent toward a large and shiny flying machine nearby. Seeing Vincent's concern,

Sambeke smiled. "It's okay. They will take us to the jet that flies us to Senegal."

Vincent followed. His wildest dreams could not imagine all he now saw: everybody wearing white man's clothes, lights so bright they made the night become day, ground made flat and hard as stone, many flying machines, small-huts as big as mountains.

Vincent noticed people staring at him. Nobody else had stretched earlobes and ear pegs through the tops of their ears. Nobody else wore toga sheets. Nobody else carried walking sticks or wore cow-skin sandals. Vincent wished he had brought his spear. He wrapped his red-striped sheet closely around his shoulders and climbed into the shiny flying machine.

"This jet will go much faster than the helicopter," Sambeke said.

Vincent nodded, working to strap himself into his seat. How could anything go faster? he wondered.

In a short while, the jet moved across the ground, making loud screaming sounds as if it were hurt. Vincent pointed out the window and spoke to Sambeke. "I do not think we are moving faster."

Sambeke laughed. "We haven't taken off yet."

Sambeke was right. Soon the flying machine made thunder, and the seat pushed at Vincent from behind. Faster and faster they moved. Vincent stiffened his legs and gripped the seat. The front of the jet tilted up, and the ground dropped away below. Vincent pressed his face against the glass and watched the lights of Nairobi fade into the night. This was truly magic.

When he could no longer see lights, Vincent shared with Sambeke the goat meat and cow's blood given to him by Peninah. "Does anything travel faster than a jet?" he asked.

Sambeke nodded. "Spaceboy Elliot travels faster than a bullet from a white man's rifle."

This Vincent did not believe. He swallowed hard—being in the flying machines made his stomach not want to hold food. Still questions filled his head, and he asked, "Sambeke, everyone in Nairobi dresses like the white man. Who are they? Are they Kikuyu, Kalenjin, or Maasai?"

"Does it matter?"

When Vincent did not answer, Sambeke smiled and asked, "Do you want to know who you can trust?"

Vincent nodded.

Sambeke held his next words before speaking. Vincent knew this made the words more important. Finally Sambeke said, "Tell me, Vincent. Do some Maasai lie and steal?"

Vincent nodded. "Yes, but that is not the way of the Maasai."

"Ah, so only good things are the ways of the Maasai. Where does the bad come from, then?" Before Vincent could answer, Sambeke continued. "The bad you see in Spaceboy Elliot, you call that the ways of the white man. Tell me, Vincent, do you have any bad in you?"

Vincent nodded.

"Then if Spaceboy Elliot sees that bad, is it the ways of the Maasai?"

Vincent did not answer.

Sambeke spoke more strongly. "If another mother had given birth to you four hundred kilometers north of here, you would be called a Somali. If your skin were white and you had been born in another land, you might have grown up with the spaceboy. You could have been his brother and worn pants that catch your gas."

"I would rather be a hyena," Vincent said, letting his voice grow angry. "Inside of me, I am Maasai!"

Sambeke smiled. "My words have touched your feelings. I think that inside you are Maasai. But also you are very much like the spaceboy. You search for what you do not know. You fear what you do not understand. I think you both look up at the same stars and ask the same questions.

"If Spaceboy Elliot were here, I would tell him the same things I tell you. I would say that you cannot hate another person without hating yourself. I think in Senegal I will discover if Vincent Ole Tome hates himself."

Vincent sat in silence. Sambeke's words were like lions—fighting them made them more dangerous. Vincent looked out at the black night. Lights below looked like the stars. This is what the world must look like to Engai. Vincent closed his eyes, but one question

224

stuck in his mind and would not let sleep steal his thoughts.

If he hated the spaceboy, was it true—did he also hate himself?

# CHAPTER TWENTY-SIX

Computer temperatures kept climbing aboard the Shuttle *Endeavour*. Shuttle pilot Victor Lutz carefully maneuvered into reentry attitude for the emergency landing. With the Orbiter faced forward, nose up at a steep angle, he announced, "Houston, this is *Endeavour*. We are in entry attitude. Over."

"Roger, in entry attitude. Houston, out."

The checklist chatter continued. "Cabin relief A and B. Antiskid, on. Nosewheel steering, off. Entry roll mode, off. Speed brake and throttle controls, full forward. Air data on auto. Hydraulic main pump pressure switches, normal. Hydraulic pressure indicators, green."

Victor Lutz spoke louder. "Houston, this is *Endeavour*. Entry switch checklist complete, over."

"Roger, *Endeavour*. Houston, out."

Commander Beaman punched keys on his computer, dumping the propellants in the forward Reaction Control System overboard. This shifted the Orbiter's balance point for reentry. He announced, "Houston, this is *Endeavour*. RCS dump complete. Over."

"Roger, *Endeavour*. Houston, out."

Elliot felt his antigravity suit tighten. Reentry would come soon.

Last-minute checks confirmed Orbiter altitude. Then at landing minus thirty minutes, the announcement came, "Houston, this is *Endeavour*. We are at entry interface. Ready for Loss Of Signal. Over."

"Roger, *Endeavour*, ready for LOS. Houston, out."

Elliot tightened his jaw. The Orbiter was fifty miles up and still traveling at more than sixteen thousand miles per hour. For the next ten or twelve minutes of reentry, the atmosphere would heat the nose tiles to three thousand degrees Fahrenheit. Elliot could already see a pink glow past the forward windows from the cocoon of heat that was forming.

Ionized particles were enveloping the Orbiter, blanking out all radio communications. The Shuttle could burn up now without Houston even knowing. Elliot felt pressure against his seat. At first he thought it was the return of gravity, but it was only the Shuttle slowing down.

The windows glowed dark orange, then fiery white. Energy from the forty-four million horsepower spent by the solid rockets at launch was still inside the Shuttle. The twenty-three Hoover Dams of energy from the main engines was still stored in the Orbiter. Now on reentry, all that energy was being given back as blistering heat. Three thousand degrees were plucking and gnawing at the Orbiter, trying to burn it up.

**AS THE NASA** jet winged its way through the dark night across northern Africa, Vincent squirmed. He looked at Sambeke sleeping hard. How could a person sleep sitting up? Were they really flying through the air faster than a bird? It didn't feel that way.

Somewhere in the night Vincent also fell asleep, his head resting against Sambeke's shoulder. He awoke hours later, stiff from sleeping upright. He squinted out from the jet's rounded window at the dark sky.

Sambeke glanced over. "Ah, Dreamer Boy awakes. We are nearing Senegal. Are you ready to meet your friend Elliot?"

Vincent scratched at his knee before answering, "Elliot is not my friend."

Sambeke smiled. "People do not understand enemies."

"You speak Peninah's words," Vincent said, looking at Sambeke. "So, you think I understand Elliot?"

Sambeke nodded. "You are beginning to understand yourself. Other people are not very different."

"Does that mean that people with enemies do not understand themselves?"

228

Sambeke smiled. "In Senegal we shall see."

Vincent stood to stretch. Sambeke's words made him angry.

One of the pilots poked his head back from the cockpit. "We are descending into Dakar. Please fasten your seatbelts."

The jet screamed less, and the front tilted downward. Vincent sat and hooked the waist strap. Staring out the window, he could not explain the fear that ate like a buzzard at his stomach.

"Something I did not tell you," said Sambeke. "When I spoke to your father, he said he would let you go to the wood school."

This surprised Vincent, but he shrugged. "That will cost three cows. Without rain, we will soon have no cows."

Sambeke spoke. "After today, there will be many ways to pay for your school. You will not need cows."

Vincent turned. "How can that be?"

"Wait and see."

Slowly Vincent allowed the wonderful thought into his mind. Could this be real? He squirmed with excitement.

Now it looked as if the lights on the ground were rising up to meet them. The ground came closer and moved faster. Vincent did not understand how this could happen. It moved so fast that Vincent closed his eyes as they landed. The jet bumped and shook. The engines roared louder than any lion. Vincent opened his eyes to watch the ground slow. The jet turned onto a big smooth path.

"We are taxiing," Sambeke said. "Welcome to Dakar."

Vincent stared hard. Many lighted small-huts could be seen. "Here they also have the bright lights that make it day!" he exclaimed. "Look at all the square small-huts. They are so big."

"That's where people work," Sambeke said.

"What work needs a small-hut as big as a mountain? Do they graze their cows inside?"

Sambeke laughed. "I think there is much I need to explain. We will have time after the Shuttle lands and after you meet Spaceboy Elliot."

Vincent saw many people near the big small-huts, like herds of cattle. He shook his head. "Sambeke," he asked, "why do these people build their small-huts so close together?"

Sambeke motioned. "Hurry, Vincent. Soon the Shuttle *Endeavour* will land."

Vincent jumped to his feet.

Several white men wearing pants and white shirts waited for Vincent and Sambeke as they left the jet. Vincent bowed his head to be touched, but the white elders would not touch his head. Instead, they smiled and held out their hands. Vincent backed away from them. What were they doing? These were not his friends! He looked to Sambeke, frightened.

"This is how they greet us," Sambeke said, reaching out to shake hands with each in the small group.

Reluctantly Vincent reached out his hand and did the same. The stranger's touch nearly stopped him from breathing. He looked down. Here, as in Nairobi, the smooth hard ground left no footprints. "Is all the ground like this in Senegal?" he asked as they followed the group of men. He kicked at the flat surface.

"This is made by people so there will be no mud."

"How can the earth know life if it is covered?"

Sambeke threw his hands up. "Dreamer Boy, save your questions. We go now to eat a quick morning meal. When the sun comes up, we will see our first Shuttle landing." Sambeke spoke more quietly. "We are guests, so we must eat whatever is given—even if it is the food of the Potato Person. Do you understand?"

Reluctantly Vincent nodded. He would try. He followed the group into one of the buildings. Many people turned to watch Vincent and Sambeke walk by in their toga sheets.

The meal was very bad. Sambeke explained the food to Vincent. There was a banana and a drink made from oranges. Nobody here drank from calabashes—they used round containers made from window glass. For the first time Vincent tasted cooked chicken eggs and hot potatoes that were also cooked. He forced down each awful swallow. This must be the kind of food that Potato Boy Elliot ate, he thought. He would have given anything for a big chunk of raw goat's liver and some cow's blood.

Obediently, Vincent picked at his food. Sambeke's

glances stopped him each time he started wrinkling his nose. One of the white men stood and looked at his watch. "The Shuttle should be entering deorbit burn by now," he said. "Let's go to the viewing area for the landing."

# CHAPTER TWENTY-SEVEN

**E**lliot watched the turbulent flow of white plasma lighting the corners of the windows. The plasma changed slowly from white to orange, to pink, then disappeared, and the window cleared. In the night, many more lights on the ground could be seen, and it was obvious now that the Shuttle was much lower.

Victor Lutz started a wide sweeping S-turn. "We should be out of communications blackout soon," he announced. His next words were, "Houston, this is *Endeavour*. Do you copy? Over."

The reply came almost instantly, "Roger, *Endeavour*, we copy. It's nice to hear you. This is Houston. All systems look good. Over."

"Roger. All systems are go. Out."

The melting of tension on the flight deck could be

felt. Space Shuttle *Endeavour* wasn't down yet, but it had come through the fiery heat of reentry in one piece. Still it traveled nearly eight thousand miles per hour. The Orbiter rumbled as speed brakes extended. Elliot watched the horizon tilt in the front windshield as they entered a second, third, and fourth S-turn.

"We're down to sixteen hundred miles per hour," Commander Beaman announced. "We're barely creeping."

Several seconds later, Victor Lutz announced, "Houston, this is *Endeavour*. Entering terminal-area energy management interface. Everything looks fine. Over."

"Roger, *Endeavour*. Houston, out."

As the Orbiter slowed subsonic, it buffeted. Elliot didn't hear it, but he knew that two deafening sonic booms had echoed outward from the wingtips. They probably scared Vincent Ole Tome.

The nose of the Orbiter lowered for final approach, and the Earth became visible again. It was very close now—less than ten thousand feet away. They came in steeply. Elliot hung forward against his shoulder straps. He knew from training they were coming in seven times steeper than an airliner, dropping faster than a sky diver in free fall. It was like the most incredible toboggan ride without snow.

"*Endeavour*, this is Houston. Have you acquired autoland? Over."

Victor Lutz answered, "Roger, Houston. Out."

Now the Orbiter slowed to barely three hundred miles per hour. It had turned itself from a spacecraft with rockets back into an airplane, except this airplane had no engines. They were gliding and had only one chance to land.

Victor Lutz pulled the nose of the Orbiter up at about two thousand feet, then spoke. "Houston, this is *Endeavour*. Preflare initiated. Over."

"Roger, *Endeavour*. Out."

For the first time, Elliot saw the runway. From this high, it looked really tiny.

*Endeavour* came in fast and ghostlike over the countryside, vapor trails spiraling off both wings. Because the ground was close now, three hundred miles per hour seemed much faster than seventeen thousand miles per hour in orbit. Victor Lutz applied full speed brake. "We're almost home!" he announced. He reached forward and lifted a panel cover. He pushed the landing gear switch.

A clunk was felt.

"*Endeavour*, this is Houston. Gear down. Over."

"Roger, gear down and locked. Out."

"*Endeavour*, this is Houston. Your main gear is at ten feet . . . five feet . . . four feet . . . three feet . . . two feet . . . one . . . contact."

Elliot braced himself and felt a bump.

"Nosewheel at five feet, four, three, two, one, contact."

Another bump.

"Roger, contact."

Elliot couldn't see the huge red, white, and blue parachute that billowed out behind the Orbiter. He did feel himself press forward against his harness. The Orbiter slowed and finally stopped. Space Shuttle *Endeavour* had returned to the planet Earth.

"*Endeavour* to Convoy One. Wheels stop. Over."

"Roger, *Endeavour*. This is Convoy One. Wheels Stop. Welcome home!"

Yellow trucks swarmed onto the runway toward the shuttle to deactivate all systems. Elliot released his harness. He tensed and tried to stand. His body felt made of lead. If he hadn't been holding the side of the seat, he would have fallen.

For the first time Elliot realized how free he had been in orbit. Not even a bird was as free as someone floating in space. Kneeling on his seat, he looked out the window. Thousands of people had gathered near the main terminal building. Military vehicles and soldiers with green uniforms lined the airfield on both sides for security.

Elliot took a deep breath. Somewhere out there was Vincent Ole Tome.

**VINCENT THANKED ENGAI** that he did not have to eat all of his morning meal. He was not yet ready to become a Potato Person. He and Sambeke followed the white people to a seating area on a large platform. Vincent started to sit directly on the platform but Sambeke motioned him onto one of the chairs.

The sky had grown lighter with the coming of the day. A soft breeze blew. Many yellow cars and trucks lined the runway, red lights flashing from their tops. Again and again the white people tried to ask Vincent questions. He nodded and grunted short replies, but he did not like talking to the strangers.

Everybody looked upward now. Vincent stared but could see only the dawn sky that had arrived. Suddenly two loud rifle shots rang out. Vincent glanced around fearfully. Had someone killed a lion?

"Those are the sonic booms from the Shuttle going subsonic," one of the white men explained.

The words made no sense to Vincent. He kept watching. He saw nothing and wondered if a big trick was being played on him. Was he really in Senegal, meeting a spaceboy named Elliot? He shook his head. It couldn't be.

"There they are!" somebody shouted. While others still searched, Vincent spotted a tiny dot crossing the sky to his left. It looked like a high-flying hawk. He gazed intently at the dot as it moved.

"Do you see it?" Sambeke asked.

Vincent nodded and pointed. "It is a jet flying machine."

"No, it's the Shuttle," Sambeke said. "It looks and flies like an airplane, but see how steep it comes down."

As the dot grew larger and took shape, two smaller dots appeared.

"The smaller dots are the chase planes that meet and follow the Shuttle," Sambeke said.

Vincent watched the dots turn toward them. Now the big white spaceship could be seen clearly. Smoke trailed from each wing. Like a great magic bird made by Engai, the white spaceship drifted silently from the sky, closer and closer. When it seemed the flying machine would hit the ground, the nose pulled up and slowed its fall. Still, white smoke curled off the wingtips.

Vincent held his hands in fists and did not breathe. He blinked. Never before had his eyes seen anything so wonderful.

The spaceship's rear tires touched the ground with puffs of smoke. Then the nose lowered slowly until the front tire also touched with a puff of smoke. The smoke faded from the wings. A great colorful piece of cloth billowed out behind the flying machine, spinning, hopping, and bouncing until the spaceship slowed. Then the big cloth broke away and collapsed on the ground. New curls of smoke rose from the side and back of the spaceship.

The crowd of people clapped and cheered. The yellow cars and trucks beside the landing strip raced toward the spaceship, their red lights flashing and sirens screaming. Vincent shivered with excitement. Still the morning sun had not shown itself above the land.

"It takes about an hour to secure the Shuttle and get medical checks," announced one of the white men, turning to Vincent. He spoke loudly enough for a whole engang to hear. "And then you'll meet your buddy, Elliot."

# CHAPTER TWENTY-EIGHT

**D**ozens of people worked around the Space Shuttle *Endeavour*, preparing for the astronauts to egress. Victor Lutz and Commander Beaman remained in their cockpit seats. Laughing now and joking freely, the rest of the crew stood and stretched their cramped muscles.

Elliot stared from the flight-deck window. In the gray dawn before sunrise, he could see crowds gathered. Nearer to the runway, a small group sat in chairs on a platform. Elliot licked at his dry lips. He wished he was meeting Mandy and not Vincent Ole Tome.

Elliot suddenly heard the words he dreaded. "Control, this is *Endeavour*. We are ready for crew egress. Over."

"Roger, *Endeavour*, ready for egress. Convoy One, this is Control. Proceed with crew egress. Over."

An arrow's shot away from the Shuttle, Vincent Ole Tome sat waiting. He stared nervously at the steps pushed alongside the white Orbiter. He could see faces look out from the windows high in the air. It was too far away to see if one of the faces was that of Spaceboy Elliot. Vincent ignored the voices asking him questions. He rubbed his cow-skin sandals against each other. The light breeze stopped blowing—even the air had held its breath.

Men in white bodysuits opened the hatch. Two woman astronauts stepped out, dressed in bright orange pressure suits. The crowd erupted with cheers. Next a man astronaut appeared. Then a boy astronaut with light-colored hair stepped into the humid Senegal air. Carefully he headed down the steps.

Focusing on the Shuttle, Vincent stood and stepped off the platform. He started toward Spaceboy Elliot. A guard tried to stop him, but one of the men from NASA motioned for the guard to let the Maasai boy pass. As if controlled by a big hand, Vincent walked forward across the big field of black ground. He held his walking stick close to his sheet.

Coming down the steps of the Shuttle, Elliot searched the crowd gathered across the tarmac. He wore his orange pressure suit. In his right hand he still held the oxygen helmet worn during reentry.

When the whole crew was on the ground, Commander Beaman pointed to the gray van waiting for them. "We'll take this van into the terminal area," he said. "After we get these orange monkey suits off, we'll have medical exams. Then we'll go over to the stage by the tarmac for welcoming ceremonies."

Everybody turned to follow Commander Beaman toward the van. That's when Elliot spotted the lone figure dressed in a bright red sheet. A solitary black-skinned boy had walked past the guards in the terminal area and was headed across the tarmac directly toward the Shuttle.

"Vincent," Elliot breathed.

Controlled by the same hand that guided Vincent, Elliot turned and walked toward the Maasai herder.

"Where are you going?" Commander Beaman called.

"It's Vincent," Elliot said. "Can I go meet him?"

Commander Beaman started to object but, seeing the boy with sandals and a walking staff heading toward them, he nodded. "They've let the boy past security, so go ahead. Make it short or you'll cook in your pressure suit."

"I'll be right back." Elliot headed deliberately out across the open space that separated him from Vincent Ole Tome.

Alone in an envelope of time and space, the two boys crossed the wide tarmac toward each other. *Endeavour*'s crew stopped beside the van to watch. Nearer the terminal, Sambeke stood and held his breath. The crowd of nearly ten thousand people hushed. Cameras from a dozen nations followed every movement as Elliot and Vincent approached each other. They stopped barely two feet apart, their faces showing no emotion.

Slightly taller than Elliot, Vincent stood with his coal black skin, his red toga sheet, colored pegs through the tops of his ears, cow-skin sandals, and a walking staff.

Elliot stood in his bulky orange pressure suit, his helmet under his arm. Big beads of sweat dotted his forehead and wet his blond hair into strands.

For a long moment neither spoke, then Vincent said quietly, "Elliot?"

Elliot nodded. "Vincent?"

Vincent nodded.

Curious smiles crept across their faces.

Vincent swallowed, then spoke. "I am glad that your god has brought you safe back to the ground."

Still they stared hard at each other.

Elliot nodded and spoke. "I'm also glad that your god, Engai, brought you here safely. Did you fly all night?"

Vincent nodded. "Your world is one of magic. You are very different."

"I'm different?" Elliot said. "Why do you have big holes and yellow pegs in your ears. What are they for?"

"The pegs and holes make me handsome."

"Handsome," Elliot said. "You're kidding."

Distrust flared in Vincent's eyes.

Elliot spoke again quickly. "I'm sorry for saying that. Commander Beaman says we're probably a lot alike but we just don't know it."

"That is what Sambeke said."

"Is he the doctor I talked to?"

"Yes, you will meet him today."

"Maybe some time I can visit Kenya, and you can show me how you live," Elliot said.

"Yes, and maybe someday I can visit the United States of America and see how you live."

They stood in awkward silence. Thumbing nervously at his walking stick, Vincent said, "Elliot, I do not think you wear pants to trap your gas."

Elliot laughed. "I'm wearing a pair of white socks that smell that way right now."

Vincent hesitated. "Elliot, will you get angry if I ask you a question?"

Elliot shook his head. "Of course not."

"Are we friends?"

"I suppose we could be . . . but we're sure different."

Vincent studied the white boy standing so close. "Yes, we are very different. But I, too, think we can be friends." Again a long and awkward silence rose like a thick wall between them.

Elliot smiled and nodded. "We should be real good friends after all that's happened. Don't you think so?"

Vincent smiled broadly. "Yes. I think we are very good friends."

Without warning, Elliot stepped forward and hugged Vincent.

Vincent pushed Elliot away. "What are you doing?" he blurted.

"You said we were friends!"

"Yes, but why do you grab me?"

"I didn't grab you—I hugged you. That's how we show we like someone in the United States," Elliot said.

Vincent paused. "If this is how you show friendship, then I will learn to show friendship in this way," Vincent said, stepping forward. Deliberately he hugged Elliot.

A cheer went up from the crowd.

Embarrassed, both boys let go and looked around. They had forgotten about the huge crowds and the cameras. On the horizon, the new sun broke into view and spilled a soft warm light across the Senegal countryside.

"Do you want to come over to the terminal with me to unsuit?" Elliot asked.

"Yes, I would like to do that."

Walking side by side, Vincent and Elliot started back toward the Shuttle *Endeavour* and toward the gray van. The whole crew stood waiting. They were clapping.

Elliot smiled. "I can't wait to have you meet everyone," he said.

"I will like that," said Vincent, taking Elliot's hand.

Elliot jerked his hand away. "We can't hold hands," he said. "We're on world television."

"But that is how *we* show friendship," Vincent said, his voice guarded.

For a moment Elliot appeared to struggle with his thoughts. Then he nodded. "If that's how the Maasai show friendship, I can learn to show friendship like that, too."

"We are friends?" Vincent asked.

"Yes, we're friends," Elliot answered.

With those simple words, on that morning in Senegal, two very different boys reached out and touched hands. Because of that moment, the future of a tiny planet named Earth, located in a distant spiral arm of a remote galaxy, glowed warmer against the cold black of a wonderful and undiscovered universe.

*"I have spoken and acted bravely
all the time, and I feel good about it.
I hope that my children will be
able to follow in my footsteps."*

—*Words of a dying Maasai elder*

**BEN MIKAELSEN** lives in Bozeman, Montana, with his wife, Melanie, and a six-hundred-pound bear named Buffy. Mr. Mikaelsen's first novel, *Rescue Josh McGuire*, was published by Hyperion in 1991 and received both the Western Writers of America Spur Award and the International Reading Association's Best First Work in the older readers category. Since then, Ben Mikaelsen has also authored *Sparrow Hawk Red* and *Stranded*.

In researching *Countdown*, Ben and Melanie travelled to Africa and lived with the Maasai near the Tanzania border, and also spent a month at the U.S. Space and Rocket center in Huntsville, Alabama.

# DATE DUE

| | | | |
|---|---|---|---|
| | | | |
| | | | |
| | | | |
| | | | |
| | | | |
| | | | |
| | | | |
| | | | |
| | | | |
| | | | |
| | | | |
| | | | |
| | | | |
| | | | |
| | | | |
| | | | |
| | | | |
| | | | |
| | | | |

FOLLETT